Isaac W. North, Leonard H. Courtney

A Week in the Isles of Scilly

Revised and rewritten by Leonard H. Courtney

Isaac W. North, Leonard H. Courtney

A Week in the Isles of Scilly
Revised and rewritten by Leonard H. Courtney

ISBN/EAN: 9783337406424

Printed in Europe, USA, Canada, Australia, Japan

Cover: Foto ©Andreas Hilbeck / pixelio.de

More available books at **www.hansebooks.com**

PENZANCE:

PRINTED BY EDWARD ROWE,

30, MARKET-PLACE.

PREFACE.

THIS Book is founded on " A Week in the Isles of Scilly," by the Rev. J. W. North, published by the present Publisher in 1850, but it has been so thoroughly re-constructed that it may be regarded as a new work. It is hoped that the alterations and additions will make the book more useful to the Visitor; but it is right to say that Mr. North, who ceased to reside in Scilly many years since, is in no way responsible for them. Any corrections will be thankfully received by the Publisher.

A WEEK IN THE ISLES OF SCILLY.

INTRODUCTORY CHAPTER.

The Scilly Islands lie W.S.W. from the Land's End at a distance of about 27 miles, but their distance from Penzance, the port of embarkation of ordinary visitors, is about 42 miles. A small but commodious screw steamer, the Little Western, makes the voyage from Penzance to Scilly thrice a week during the Summer months, and twice a week during the Winter; the passage usually occupying about four hours. The fares are 6s. and 3s. 6d.; return-tickets are not issued except on special excursions, but it may be questioned whether the proprietors of the steamer would not consult their own interest in issuing return-tickets to tourists. Some of our readers may remember Mr. Walter White's hungry experience on board the former sailing packet, the Lionesse, ("A Londoner's Walk to the Land's End,") and we therefore add that refreshments can be procured from the Steward of the Little Western. At St. Mary's, the largest island, there are several inns; the best is kept by the master of the Little Western, Captain Tregarthen; others are kept by Mumford, Duff, Hicks, and Ellis. There are also some very good lodging-houses where visitors can obtain fair attendance, at moderate charges. Besides St. Mary's, four other islands, Tresco, St. Martin's, St. Agnes, and Bryher, are inhabited, and till lately two or three families lived on Sampson; their acreage and population are shewn in the following table.

B

Acres.			Population.				
Heath's estimate.	1750		1822*	1831	1841	1851	1861
St. Mary's	1640		1400	1311	1545	1668	1532
Tresco	880		480	470	430	416	399
St. Martin	720	1400 Heath's estimate	280	230	214	211	185
St. Agnes	390		282	289	243	204	200
Bryher	330		140	128	121	118	115
Sampson	120		34	37	29	10	none
			2616	2465	2582	2627	2431

* Woodley's estimate.

Rabbits breed plentifully on some dozen smaller islands, and in summer cattle find a little pasture upon them. Of rocky islets and rocks there is an innumerable quantity. The tourist who wishes to pass from St. Mary's to the other islands, (called by the inhabitants the Off Islands) will of course require a boat and a boatman, or boatmen : we should advise him to engage these as soon as possible : the islanders, from causes which we shall hereafter explain are so prosperous that few care to seek the casual gains of keeping boats for hire ; those who do so are Duff (whom we can recommend,) Obadiah Hicks, James Nicholas, and Samuel Jenkins. The usual charge for a good boat is half-a-crown a day, and as much for each man hired with it ; for a small boat and one man the charge is about four shillings a day. The tourist should take materials for luncheon with him.

As the voyage from Penzance to Scilly always takes place in the day-time, and the steamer in ordinary weather keeps close to the shore for the first part of the way, this chapter may not improperly conclude with a notice of the objects seen on the passage. From Penzance the steamer stretches across that part of Mount's Bay called Gwavas Lake, at the head of which is the village of Newlyn, towards Penlee the southern arm of the Lake. The best view of Penzance and the hills behind it is seen during this part of the course. After leaving Penlee, the tourist sees the village of Mouse-hole, and Mousehole Island, otherwise called St. Clement's, a chapel having formerly stood on it dedicated to that Saint. Next a cavern appears, from which, as the mouse's hole, a vulgar error derives the name of the village. Presently the vessel passes the entrance to Lamorna, a picturesque little valley, some of the beauty of which is however marred by the quarrying works and landing stage of the Messrs. Freeman. The next headland but one is surmounted by a pile of rocks called Carn Boscawen, and forms one horn of St. Loy's Cove, above which are seen the woods of Boskenna, the seat of the Paynter family. Penberth Cove follows, on the West of which are the rocks of Castle Treryn and the Logan Rock. Next is the Rundle Stone, a rock visible at half-tide and marked by a buoy; and a little to the N. W. is Tol Pedn Penwith, a fine bold promontory and the most southerly point of the peninsula of the Land's End. Here the steamer leaves the neighbourhood of the shore and steers across the mid-ocean to Scilly, but the coast of the Land's End and Cape Cornwall, and the Longships lighthouse, a little more than a mile West of the Land's End, remain visible for some time. In fine weather the village and church of Sennen are also distinctly seen. The steamer's course lies over the site of the fabled Lyonness where

> ..All day long the noise of battle roll'd
> Among the mountains by the Winter sea ;
> Until King Arthur's table, man by man,
> Had fallen in Lyonness about their lord.

This submerged country is said to have contained 140 parish churches ; but there is no reason whatever for accepting the tradition ; and, although the geography of the Arthurian legends is confused and contradictory, it is tolerably certain that the Lyonness mentioned in them is the district of the Leonnois in Brittany. Soon after the steamer stands out to sea, it passes on the South, the Wolf Rock, on which a lighthouse is now in course of erection. Although the Scilly Islands may be easily discerned in fine weather from the Land's End, they lie too low to be seen from the deck of the little steamer until the passage is half accomplished, when a day-mark on 'the nearest island,

St. Martin's, makes its appearance and almost simultaneously with it the light-ship of the Seven Stones, a group of rocks about seven miles to the North-east of St. Martin's. If the islands be reached at the time of high water, the steamer will pass through Crow Sound between St. Martin's and St. Mary's, having the latter island on its left or Southern side, but at other times the depth of water in this Sound is not sufficient, and the longer course to the South of St. Mary's and thence Northwards through St. Mary's Sound, must be taken. Supposing Crow Sound to be passable, the steamer's course before entering it lies close to the South side of a group called the Eastern Islands ; whilst approaching them, a high conical rock called Hanjague, is conspicuous on the North, but it is soon lost amongst its fellows. Of these islands a more particular account will be found in the excursion to St. Martin's. Meanwhile that island itself is passed on the right, and then Tresco is seen, and on it the Abbey, the residence of Mr. A. Smith, M.P., the Lessee of the islands. On St. Mary's a beautiful heath-clad hill is passed, and next a fine mass of rocks called Carn Morval ; just as the steamer enters the Port, St. Agnes, with its lighthouse, is seen to the South West, and a little to the right, in the distance, the lighthouse on the Bishop Rock. The longer course, which as we have said must be adopted at low water, runs around the South of St. Mary's, passing Porthellick, where the body of Sir Cloudesley Shovel was washed ashore, and soon after rounding Peninis, the finest headland in the islands. St. Agnes, with its lighthouse, is then passed on the left, and the Peninsula, crowned with the Star Castle, on the right, immediately after which the steamer comes to an anchor in the Pool. The Pier at which the passengers land was built in the years 1835-8 : it juts out from the back of the former pier, which still remains to show how meagre was the accommodation it afforded. The visitor being thus landed at St. Mary's we shall break off this chapter, only adding, for his information, if he be pressed for time, that the objects best worth seeing are :—

St. Mary's. The walk around the Garrison, *i. e.,* the

Star Castle, and the Peninsula occupied by it and its batteries. The Rocks at Peninnis.

Tresco. The Abbey Gardens. Oliver's Castle and the New Grimsby Harbour.

St. Agnes. The Light House.

The Bishop Rock and Light House. Castle Bryher. Round Island. Menavawr. But those who can afford the time may 'easily devote a day or more to each of the following excursions.

NOTES ON THE NAMES OF PLACES IN SCILLY.

The greater number of the names of places in Scilly are pure Cornish. The first class of exceptions contains those due to the influence of the church; the principal Islands are named after the Saints to whom their churches or oratories have been dedicated,—St. Mary's, St. Martin's, St. Sampson's, St. Helen's, (or rather St. Elid's) and Tean (St. Theona). Tresco was for a time called St. Nicholas' Island, and St. Warna has given her name to one or two parts of St. Agnes. *St.* Agnes we have written in accordance with usage, but the prefix is a mistake; this Island's name is properly Agnes, Hagenes, or Hagness, it is so written in a series of records commencing in the reign of Richard I (*Rot. Cur. Regis ed. Palgrave I*, 80), and in a map certainly drawn before 1580 it is called Angnes (*Cott. MSS., Aug. I, II,* 18). Agnes and Grimsby, the harbour of Tresco, are probably relics of the time when the Northmen used those Islands as a station. The next class of names not Cornish, contains places called after former owners, *e. g.*, Toll's Island, Bab's Carn (Carn,—pile of rocks), Buzza's Hill, and similar to these are Frenchman's Grave, Dutchman's Carn, &c., which probably commemorate some unhappy shipwrecked strangers. Such names as Rat Island, Puffin Island, Rushy Bay, &c., need no explanation. The names of Cornish origin shew a tendency to a soft pronunciation; the names in the county itself lack the roughness of the corresponding Welsh or Breton forms, but in Scilly they are still smoother. Thus Porth, a bay, is reduced to Por or Per, Permellin, Porcrasa, &c.; Trescaw (scaw, an alder,) is softened into Tresco ; Gwynheli, in Cornwall Goonhilly, is in Scilly Ganilly ; Menawidden is changed into Menawethan, Treanmen into Trenemen, Enys-an-geon into Innisidgen, Enys-withek into Inniswilgie and even Illiswithick. In the same spirit a vowel is frequently inserted between the component parts of a name, as Carne̷wethers, Crebawethan, Carnifriers, Menawethan, &c. When we proceed to single names we must confess that we are often baffled ; for *Scilly* itself, derivations from *sylly*, a conger-eel, *scylly*, to separate, *skoly* or *skuly*, to scatter, *sul-leh*, a suu-rock, have been suggested, but none of them is satisfactory. — As our limits will not allow us to discuss separate names, we must conclude by impressing on the reader one universal law of composition, and by giving him a few common words. The law is that the general name always precedes the special descriptive name, or in other words the noun-substantive comes first and the noun-adjective second,—thus in Peninis, pen is head and inis is island, but Peninis means the island-head and not the head-island. For common words we may give in addition to Carn. Porth or Por, Pen, and Inis or Enys already explained; Creeb, or Creb a crest, Men, a rock, Bre, a hill, Tre, a homestead.

[*A Paper on this subject, read by Mr. Edwin Norris, the Editor of the* "Cornish Drama," *before the Cambrian Archæological Association, is printed in the* "Arch. Camb.," *Jan.* 1863.]

FIRST EXCURSION.

Sampson, Bryher, and Adjacent Islets.

Our first excursion shall be to Sampson and Bryher. Steering across the Road in a Westerly course, for the former of these islands, we pass at a distance of three quarters of a mile from it and about the same distance from Tresco, the conspicuous Nut Rock, the mark for pilots bringing vessels to the, main anchorage. Those two hills before you, to the most Southerly of which we will direct our boat, are the Isle of Sampson. You will find a convenient landing-place on the Eastern side of the island.

Two or three writers have supposed that Sampson and Bryher were formerly united, and have referred to some doubtful evidence in support of the hypothesis. The depth of water between the two islands makes the suggestion wholly improbable. Sampson may have been united at one time to Tresco, as it is possible at low water to wade, from one island to the other; and for a similar reason Tresco, may have been joined to Bryher.

Sampson had formerly from thirty to forty inhabitants, but it was deemed advisable to remove them, as opportunities offered, to St. Mary's, that the parents might have greater facilities for gaining their livelihood, and that the children might enjoy the benefits of education. No one now lives on the island, and a visit to the roofless cottages will show that the change was on every account desirable.

Ascending the highest point of land, you will gain a commanding view of the Isles, and, at one glance, take in their relative situation and proportions. St. Mary's is seen to great advantage with its Church and harbour, the Garrison surmounted by the Star Castle; St. Agnes with its distinguishing feature, the Light-house ; Annet stretching out towards the West, with its jaggy extremities, like so many hay-cocks ; and, over the outer-most point of Annet, the Bishop Rock crowned by its elegant Light-house.

The rock which stands nearly due West from Sampson is Minearlo ; those more to the South are Little and Great Minalto. That most to the West is Maiden Bower ; and to the North of Maiden Bower ;stands the rock which has given its name to this our English Archipelago. For the speculations on the origin of this name we refer to the note to our introductory chapter.

Scilly is a flat islet of massive rock, divided into two parts by a deep chasm, through which the water flows. Each part is surmounted by a small lump of rock, styled the North and South Cuckoo. It is with great difficulty that a landing is affected on Scilly or on any of the neighbouring rocks, from the strong tides which run between them. It can be accomplished only when the weather has been for some time very calm.

Between Maiden Bower and Sampson are the Seal Rock, Inniswilgic, and Castle Bryher. The last rock is a conspicuous feature in the scenery, and arrests attention whenever the eye is turned in that direction. Its bold and rugged summit rises finely above the low lands of Sampson and is seen from The Road and almost every island of the group. Between the isle of Bryher and Scilly is an uncultivated islet, called Gweal, containing seven acres.

From this picturesque group of rocks the eye will quickly travel to Bryher, with its White Church, and Tresco, with Oliver Cromwell's Castle. Having thus surveyed this portion of the group of Islands, the visitor may rejoin his boat, and if the wind and tide permit, approach to Castle Bryher and the other rocks, in the midst of which it stands. Castle Bryher rises to a height of 96 feet 3 inches above the sea level. Maiden Bower is a fine bold rock, and Scilly is acknowledged to deserve the name of au Isle.

From these outstanding rocks and isles the visitor should make for the Northern promontory of Bryher, called Shipman Head. By taking this course he will leave unnoticed the Southern and South Western portions of this Isle. He may not deem it necessary minutely to inspect every bay or promontory; more especially as the prospect from the Town Hill will sufficiently show the chief objects of interest. For the benefit, however, of those who neither lack time nor inclination to make the complete circuit of Bryher, we will give a more particular description of its various parts.

The Southern Hill is called Sampson Hill; and the bay which lies nearly due South on the Western side of this hill is marked in the map, Rushy Bay. This appears a more reasonable name than Russia Bay, by which it is mentioned in Woodley's history; for which he very properly says, " it were vain to enquire the reason." Doubtless the name was suggested by the growth of rushes on that part of the island.

The bay, which lies at the West South West corner, is Stony Bay; deriving its name from the shingle* with which its beach is covered. Colvel Rocks are in a line with the Southern promontory by which this bay is terminated, and Heath Point is its Northern, or rather North Western, boundary.

Between Heath Point and the next high land, which is Gweal Hill, so named from the islet lying opposite to it, is Long Bay, commonly called Great Porth. At low spring tides you may easily walk from Bryher to Gweal.

Near the Northern extremity of Great Porth, and to the East of Gweal Hill, is a lake or pond of fresh water, covering a space of about two acres, but subject to brackishness by the spray of the sea.

There is also a spring of fresh water in the North West part of the Island, which issues out of the cliff on the sea shore. This spring (the only stream of fresh water on the

* Small, smooth stones.

c

Island) is remarkable for its purity, and is often resorted to by those who are suffering from wounds or sores. Its sanative power is generally understood and acknowledged. The bay itself is also worth visiting ; nor must we omit to notice the peculiarity, which both Troutbeck and Woodley have mentioned, that " upon this spring the sun never shines."

The Western shore of Bryher presents to those, who view it from the water, a great variety of scenery, in a succession of high lands separated from each other by deep bays. The cliff is very bold at Shipman Head, but you may conveniently land, on either the Southern or the Eastern side. The South East side is the best. The rocks which form this head-land deserve a close examination. The outer extremity of Bryher is separated from its main-land by a yawning chasm called the Gulf. Its sides are nearly perpendicular, and at the narrowest part it is only about twelve feet wide. The highest point of Shipman Head is upwards of sixty feet.

The Northern hill of Bryher, which Troutbeck describes as " the roughest and most mountainous of all the Scilly Islands," offers a very uneven surface, and but a dreary walk to the pedestrian. He may, therefore, well avoid it, and make his way along the Eastern, or, more correctly, the North Eastern side of the Island. This side of Bryher and the Western coast of Tresco form the harbour of New Grimsby. The Rock, which when viewed from a distance, seems to stand nearly in the middle of the channel, but which may be reached on foot from Bryher at low water, is called Hangman Isle ; from the circumstance, as Troutbeck tells us, that some mutinous soldiers were hanged there by the Parliament forces in the great rebellion. Nearly opposite upon the shore of Tresco stands Cromwell's Castle, which is kept in substantial repair by the Board of Ordnance.

The walk along the coast of Bryher in a Southerly direction offers a continual succession of fine views. Large masses of rock project from the Cliff, overhanging New

Grimsby, and at its base is a path, which will presently bring you to the foot of the Watch Hill. This should be ascended, as from its summit is gained a fine, extensive prospect, embracing in great measure, the objects which were seen from Sampson; but from the change of situation they appear in a somewhat different aspect. To the North, Hangman Isle, New Grimsby Harbour, and Cromwell's Castle; towards the East, St. Martin's; and about ten leagues distant, the Land's End. In the same direction, but nearer at hand, the Abbey Grounds, and the pond of fresh water; Southward, the Eastern Isles with their pretty green slopes even to the water's edge; St. Mary's, with the white sands of Crow Bar, fill up the outline; descending from the hill, a good road conducts to the Church, near which you may re-embark for St. Mary's.

A careful examination of the Eastern shore of Bryher is recommended to those, who are desirous of adding to their collection of shells.

SECOND EXCURSION

TRESCO AND ADJACENT ISLETS.

This day we propose to visit Tresco and the Isles between it and St. Martin's. We will land on the Southern beach of Tresco, at some point of the white sands, Eastward of the Abbey. In the course thither we pass a fine rock called The Mare, from its resemblance to the head and neck of a colossal horse. It is connected with some ledges, running out towards the North East, which are visible at low water. In the same direction may be observed a bold rock which wears the appearance of a crown. It forms the Southern extremity of Pentle Bay. The Northern extremity of this bay is called the Lizard Point. Pentle Bay is the best place on the shores of Tresco for shells. But for the present we must defer our visit to its beautiful sands.

A good road has recently been made from the beach on which we have landed to the Abbey grounds, offering to conduct us to the margin of those large pools of fresh water, which are so singular and beautiful a feature in the scenery of this Isle. Near them, upon an eminence, stands the Abbey. Mr. Smith very generously throws open his gardens and grounds to all visitors. Pass through the gate, which is nearly at the end of the road, and ascend the slope which lies before you, having the Abbey on your left, and the plantations on your right hand. You thus arrive at the principal entrance. Passing through the arch-way, you will be at once struck with the view, and will readily believe that the spot chosen by the Proprietor for his residence, is the best which the Islands afford. From the terrace in the front of the house, he commands the Road and all the principal Sounds ; and from the hill on which his flag-staff is placed, he sees the whole extent of his domains, North and South, East and West.

On entering the gardens you will be charmed with the gay profusion of flowers, some creeping on the ground, and others climbing the rock-work, which gives at once shelter from the winds, and opportunities of display. The climate is most favourable to vegetation, the soil is not so good, but it is probable that a greater variety of plants and flowers is found here growing in the open air, than in any other part of Great Britain. Among them we may notice the numerous tribe of Mesembrianthemums, spreading in the greatest luxuriance and beauty ; Fuchsias of all kinds, Heliotropes, Crassulas, Egyptian Arams, and the graceful Clianthus. These, and many other yet more curious plants, flourish in this genial climate, requiring only shelter and protection from the violence of gales. The Geraniums and Myrtles, and sweet scented Verbena, grow to the dimensions of considerable trees ; and, later in the year, the gardens are adorned with handsome bunches of Chrysanthemums. But the assemblage of Dracœnas will soon be the most striking object in the gardens ; they grow in the open air with great vigour and healthfulness. In the midst of the gardens stand the walls of the Old Abbey Church, mantled over with the evergreen Geranium. Troutbeck says " this Church is ninety feet in length, and thirty feet in breadth, and stands due East and West. In the South side wall is a fine arch of good workmanship ; and on the North side has been another arch, directly opposite to it, and of the same breadth, which is now fallen down, and only six feet in height standing. The Church appears, from these two arches fronting each other, to have been built in the form of a cross. The arch that is standing on the South side is twelve feet wide at the bottom, and runs up to a sharp point at the top, which is sixteen feet high ; and on the

West side of the standing arch is an arched door." Troutbeck's account of the Abbey Church is in many respects inaccurate. The dimensions of the Church are eighty feet in length, by thirty feet in breadth. The arch would indeed lead to the supposition that transepts had formed part of the original design, but there is nothing whatever in the foundation or other part of the building to show that the design had been carried into effect; and Mr. Smith is of opinion, after a careful examination, that there never was a transept. The stone used in the building is granite, excepting the arches, which are cased with a remarkably fine grit-stone of a reddish colour, supposed to have been procured from Normandy. The interior of the nave was used by the inhabitants as their burial place until the last thirty years since which period the dead have been interred in the ground around the Church. The graves remain, and are covered in questionable fashion with evergreens and flowers. It may be doubted whether it would not be better to preserve somewhat of the original character of the building, by keeping it separate from the gardens within which it stands. The monastic establishment to which this Church was attached was coeval with the Norman Conquest, but as early as the reign of Henry the First it became a cell of the Abbey of Tavistock. It was dedicated to St. Nicholas, whence Tresco, for some time, bore a second name of St. Nicholas's Island.

Returning from the gardens you will pursue your walk along the road which leads to the village. On the right lies one of the beautiful pools of fresh water, before mentioned, containing a large quantity of eels and tench. The two ponds cover a space of fifty acres. Straight before you is Shipman Head, which is seen to great advantage. As you proceed you will observe, on the opposite side of the pond a handsome group of rocks perched on the hill, which rises with a gentle acclivity from the margin of the water. The hills of Bryher, explored yesterday, soon open on your left hand, and you will recognize some of the rocks to which attention was then directed. The road now skirts the edge of the harbour, and leads by a most pleasant route in the direction of Oliver Cromwell's Castle.

The group of cottages on your right is called the Palace from a house of public entertainment formerly kept there. A little beyond them is a convenient place of landing or of embarcation in New Grimsby. The cliff rises somewhat abruptly on the right ; and masses of rock, some large and some small, protrude from its green surface. The road does not extend the whole way to the Castle, but it is continued by an easy path which leads to it.

The tower is an excellent piece of masonry, " about one hundred and sixty feet in circumference, and sixty feet high. The walls are twelve feet thick, and raised on arches. The roof is flat and has a battery of nine-pounders with a parapet wall about six feet thick. These might be employed with great effect in case of emergency, as the situation commands the harbour in every direction. At the foot of this building is a stone platform, next the sea, having also a good parapet wall upon which some old iron guns are planted." †

Above this tower, on the top of the hill, and at a height of 155 feet above mean water, are the remains of another fort, called Charles's Castle. A small piece of the original wall is distinctly visible ; and in it are one or two embrasures. Adjoining it are the ruins of a small out-work. Near this spot about eighteen years ago an earthen-ware pot was discovered, together with some pieces of money.

The view from this point will at once arrest attention. Southwards is the prospect of the channel between Tresco and Bryher. Hangman Isle lies immediately below. The hills of Bryher and its pretty bays are on your right ; St. Agnes is seen in the distance; the Garrison and St. Mary's somewhat nearer, and many other isles and rocks, with which your eye is now familiar. This is a scene of great interest and beauty in clear, fine weather.

† Drew.

Nor is it less so in the season of storm and tempest.
When the wind has for some time prevailed from the North
West, the sea rolls finely in upon the rocks at the back of
Shipman Head ; wave after wave, literally mountain high,
breaking upon the iron-bound coast, present a scene of
great magnificence and awe.

We will now leave this spot and bend our steps across
the Downs to Piper's Hole, which is at the North East
point of the Island. It is a work of some toil and
difficulty to explore this curious cavern ; and the services of
two or more of the islanders must be engaged, who will
provide a small boat and candles for your use. Some blue
lights will also be required for the purpose of a thorough
inspection of the cavern. You must be content to clamber
over fragments of rock and stones for some distance ; but,
with the assistance of an experienced guide, you will easily
surmount all obstacles and reach a pool of fresh water,
when the boat will be called in requisition. The pool
varies a good deal in its length and depth, at the different
seasons of the year. The distance across it, which may be
called its length, is generally between twelve and twenty
fathoms. If there are more than sixteen fathoms of water
it is impossible for visitors to be ferried over it. But this
is very rarely the case in the Summer months, when the
water has been reduced to *even ten* fathoms. Assuming
then that you have been able to cross the pool, you again
land, and by the aid of the candles and the blue lights gain
some idea of the extent of the cave. Its inner recess is
about one hundred fathoms from the entrance.

Woodley tells us that " there are two other remarkable
caverns at the North end of Tresco, one of which is about
twelve feet high, three feet wide, and seventy feet long, the
other is twenty feet high, ten feet wide, and above two
hundred feet long." These dimensions, in the latter case
at all events, appear to be considerably exaggerated, and it
is doubtful whether these caverns are worth visiting.
Woodley is, however, quite right in saying, " On the
North West side of the hill, and about three hundred yards

from Piper's Hole, is a cavern, called The Gun, the length of which is about sixty feet, where there is a spring of fresh water called the Gun-well, constantly running."

From Piper's Hole there is a pleasant walk along the head of Gimble Bay, called Gimble Porth by the islanders. The waves roll finely in upon the bar of sand, and break around the base of Golden Ball, Menavawr and the other rocks, which are seen from this Northern part of Tresco. From Gimble Bay you must retrace your way to the Beacon and the Town Hill, and thence to the Flag Staff, which is planted on the hill at the back of the Parsonage.

The view from the summit of this hill must not be omitted in a description of the beauties of Tresco. The larger pond of fresh water, the Abbey, the fields and the meadows ; and in an opposite direction. Sampson and Bryher, and the waters of New Grimsby are seen to great advantage.

Returning to the road, a few paces will bring you to that part of the village called the ᶜDolphin ; possibly an abbreviation of the name of the noble family of Godolphin, so long lessees of these islands. In this central spot stands the Church, a convenient and comfortable building, in the form of a cross. Near it are the Schools ; the Infant School, recently erected, is about as far from the Church in the direction towards the Abbey, as the school for the elder children is in the direction of Old Grimsby, the harbour on the North Eastern side of this island.

The Parsonage commands a good view of this part of the parish. The Dolphin fields are as good land as any in the island. Borlase with his usual accuracy has thus noticed them ; " the soil is so very fruitful, that one field of seven acres has been in tillage every year since the remembrance of man, and carries exceeding plentiful crops."

Pursuing the road towards the harbour you will pass upon your left hand some excellent gardens, which have within the last few years been allotted by the Proprietor to some of his tenants who occupy the cottages by the roadside.

Near them the Agent for the Trinity House, who also holds other important offices, resides ; and a good house has been built for the Master of the Light-Ship at the Seven Stones.* This house is most conveniently situated ; for from the high ground above it he can see the vessel which is entrusted to his charge. On this island dwellings are provided for all the men connected with the Light-Ship, that they may be under the immediate superintendence of their officers.

The harbour of Old Grimsby is overhung by a cliff, fifty feet in height. Its northern extremity is Merchant's Point ; and the several fragments of rock which jut out here and there are called Permellin Carn, Permellin Rock, and Merchant's Rock. On the Southern point of the harbour is the Old Blockhouse, "twenty eight feet in length, and twenty two feet in breadth."† This battery, if put into an efficient state, would be a serviceable means of defence to the harbour in time of war. There is, at present, only one gun.

At this part of the island, the visitor should again embark at the Pier which he will find convenient for his use, and sail in a Northerly course. The appearance of the little bay from the sea is pretty. The first islet which is passed is Northwithiel ; and steering to the South of Golden Ball, which is nearly joined to St. Helen's by a ridge of rocks, the visitor will approach Menavawr, the finest rock in these seas. On this he must land, if it be practicable. The most accessible part of the rock is at the South West end. If he is so fortunate as to effect a landing, he will find it not so difficult as it at first-sight appears, to mount its abrupt and precipitous sides. From the boat it seems to afford an inaccessible retreat to the wild birds which here lay their eggs in great number. But there is no danger in the attempt to clamber up its rugged surface. With the help of a friendly hand you may easily reach the top, which is one hundred and thirty-

---

* For a fuller notice of the Seven Stones, see the Fourth Excursion.

† Troutbeck.

nine feet above the level of the sea. Menavawr is distinguished by three high peaks, of which one is separated from the other two by a rift or chasm, through which at high water and in very calm weather a boat may shoot. There is, indeed, a channel between the other parts of this rock. John Ellis, the Proprietor's chief boatman, is said to be the only man in Scilly who has ventured to take a boat through this second channel.

When the visitor has sufficiently explored the rugged sides and highest points of Menavawr, he should re-embark and desire the helmsman to steer round it. Viewed from the water on its Northern side it is peculiarly grand.

Leaving this rock you should sail to Round Island, where the Puffins breed ; its sides are bold and rugged, and though less striking than Menavawr, it exceeds it in height, its highest point being one hundred and fifty-seven feet, five inches above mean water, or eighteen feet above Menavawr.

From the Round Island the boatman may steer through the gap into St. Helen's Pool. The island from which these waters derive their name, appears to have been formerly inhabited. Troutbeck says " There are the ruins of a church upon this island, which is the most ancient Christian building in all the Islands. It consists of a South aisle twenty one feet and six inches long, by fourteen feet and three inches wide, from which two arches, low and of an uncouth style, open into a North aisle, twelve feet wide, by nineteen feet and six inches long. There are two windows in each aisle formed in the most rustic manner ; and there is a stone jutting out, near the Eastern window in the North aisle like a platform, on which, it is supposed by some, the image of the saint stood to whom the church was dedicated." St. Helen's appears to have been erroneously substituted for St. Elid's, which is the name in all the old charters. Leland no doubt refers to it when he speaks of " St. Lyde's Isle when in times past at her (?) sepulchre was great superstition." It is difficult to speak now with any certainty as to the buildings formerly standing on this interesting isle. There is a small portion

of the original wall yet remaining ; but the far greater
part of that now standing is evidently of very recent
erection, being loosely put together without cement of any
kind.

St. Helen's is uncultivated, and the only building upon it
is the Pest House, which is opened to receive patients from
vessels under quarantine.   Goats and deer seem to claim
the island as their domain.   These animals watch from
the higher points of rock those who land upon their
territory, and are ill at ease until they see them again
retiring to their boat.   The visitor will do well to make the
circuit of this isle.   There are many fine masses of rock
upon it.   Those immediately above the Pest House principally deserve notice ; but others towards the North are
exceedingly bold.   The highest point is one hundred and
forty feet above mean level of the sea.   On the Northern
side of the isle, directly opposite Round Island, there is a
fine chasm in the rocks, through which the sea rushes with
great force, finding for itself a channel of scarcely less than
one hundred and fifty feet in length.   This place it is
worth while to explore.   On the isle, just above the
innermost recesses of the chasm, is a little chamber richly
adorned with Asplenium Marinum.

Menavawr is seen to great advantage from St. Helen's ;
and as you walk along the North West side of the isle, and
look towards New Grimsby, the houses in that part of Tresco,
with the boats and vessels riding peacefully on those calm
waters, and the rocks and islets in every direction, present
a scene of beauty and of interest scarcely inferior to any
which the Isles afford.

The opposite shores of Tean,† between St. Helen's and
St. Martin's, next invite your attention.   The shape of
this island is very irregular ; and it has consequently
several beautiful bays.   On the North side of the island
there is a chasm in the rock similar to that in White Island,
but much smaller.   Mr. Smith has converted this isle into

---

† A dissyllable, Te-an : the name is derived from St. Theona, to
whom the island was dedicated.

a preserve of white rabbits. " Here " writes Mr. Woodley " are several remarkable carns. Near one of these (called Yellow Carn) are the vestiges of a Druidical circle. Great Hill is a lofty eminence of singular abruptness, especially towards the North. A high rock called Penbrose (from the Cornu-British appellation Pedn Brauze, signifying the high head land) lies about fifty yards to the North of this Island. The passage between Tean and St. Martin's is called Tean Sound. It is studded with rocks and ledges on each side, but has a good depth of water in the middle, and may be safely used by a skilful pilot."

From the high ground of Tean the Light Ship at the Seven-Stones is distinctly seen in clear weather. Beyond it Eastward, the Land's End. Towards Tresco, the Harbour of Old Grimsby and St. Helen's Pool : on your left is St. Martin's ; and at its Southern extremity the pretty group of the Eastern Isles. Far away to the West is St. Agnes and Annet ; while nearer in the same direction lies the coast of St. Mary's, and the harbour ; the Pier and the Garrison. Here is a combination of objects similar to that seen from Bryher, and yet so different in their relative situation that the prospect has all the charms of variety, if not of novelty.

From this isle the visitor may return to St. Mary's. Direct the helmsman to take the boat sufficiently near to the Hedge Rock, in your course to the Pool, to give you a good view of its form and dimensions

THIRD EXCURSION.

St. Agnes and the Western Islets.

We propose as the object of this excursion, St. Agnes and the Western Islets. The tourist should consult his boatman as to the state of the tide, before determining whether St. Agnes shall be the first or the last point in this excursion.

Supposing the latter course adopted, the visitor will have a pleasant sail to the Bishop. At a distance about two miles from Annet Head lies Crebawethan ; and almost united with it towards the West is another islet distinguished by the name of Little Crebawethan. It was upon these rocks that the " Douro " was wrecked on the 28th January, 1843, and all her crew perished.

To the North of Crebawethan, where the waves are breaking, is the Gunner ; and, yet further in the same direction, the Nundeeps, rocks which make the passage through Broad Sound hazardous to those who are inexperienced in these seas. On the 21st of November in the same year in which the "Douro" was lost, a schooner from Smyrna, bound to London, struck upon the Gunner. She became a total wreck. The vessel and cargo were all lost. The crew took to their boat ; and, through God's mercy, safely reached Bryher, *in the night.*

There is no danger in approaching the Bishop after you have passed between Crebawethan and Round Rock which lies a little to the North West; though unless the weather is very fine and calm, it will be a matter of great difficulty and of some risk to land upon it. The position of the Light-house is certainly as picturesque as it is perilous and solitary.

The first attempt to build a Light-house on the Bishop was made in 1849 ; a building was raised, formed of cast-iron columns, sunk in the rock, and braced and stayed by wrought-iron rods. It was completed up to the Lanthorn, but before that was added, the whole edifice was swept away during a severe gale on the night of the 6th of February, 1850, the cast-iron pillars snapped off under the combined force of wind and waves. After this catastrophe, the Corporation of the Trinity House built the present Light-house of granite, which was completed and lit for the first time on the 1st of September, 1858. The Light-house Commissioners who visited it in 1859 speak of the building as " magnificent and perhaps the most exposed in the world." In rough weather the spray goes over the top of the Light-house one hundred and ten feet, and the head keeper who has been in both Eddystone and Longships, thinks the sea worse here, though not much worse. The light is dioptric† differing in this respect from St. Agnes Light, which is managed by a system of reflectors. At the top is a bell worked by machinery, to serve as a fog-signal. The cost of the illuminating apparatus was £1313 10s., that of the tower, its fittings, and the buildings on the mainland used by the light-keepers, £36,559 18s. 9d.

At a distance of one mile and a half from the Bishop, in a Northerly direction, are the Crim Rocks. They lie a very little more to the West; but the Light placed upon the Bishop gives sufficient notice of the presence of danger, to warn vessels coming in that direction.

---

† There are eight refractors of 8 to the circle ; with 19 zones of prisms, 13 above and 6 below the refractors ; fountain 4 concentric wick lamp, with regulating condenser.

From the Bishop direct your boat towards Rosevear, noting as you sail along, the ledges and shoals and rocks which abound in these seas, and which have made the Isles of Scilly an object of such great terror. The best course will be to sail Eastwards to Crebawethan, so far returning in the track you came. The swell of the Western sea makes it difficult and hazardous to sail towards the South of Rosevear from the Bishop. As soon as you have passed Crebawethan, steer South South East, and you will soon see Jacky's Rock, memorable for the wreck of " The Thames" steamer, on the morning of the 4th of January, 1841, when on her passage from Dublin to London. The weather at the time was most unfavourable to any attempt to render assistance. When the calamity was discovered by the pilots on St. Agnes, the wind was blowing North West to North North East, with heavy storms of hail and rain mingled with snow. It was, therefore, impossible to afford any effectual aid; and out of sixty-five persons only four were saved. The records kept at the Light-house on St. Agnes preserve the remembrance of other shipwrecks on these dangerous rocks, not perhaps so awfully fatal, but accompanied with great loss of life.

The long reef of rocks at your side is called " The Ponds. " Rosevear is still to the South, separated from The Ponds by a channel called Santaspery Neck. Upon a rock close by this Neck, a schooner belonging to Plymouth and laden with wheat, struck on the 27th of March, 1840. She became a total wreck ; but the crew were happily saved and brought on shore by some of the intrepid inhabitants of St. Agnes. From Rosevear you will be glad to survey at leisure the isles and rocks in the midst of which it stands. On it were erected the temporary dwellings of the workmen engaged in building the Light-house on the Bishop. The trouble of walking and scrambling over Rosevear will be repaid by a nearer view of the masses of rock which lie around, and which the waters of the great Western ocean are continually chafing.

The Dutch barque, " Nubicto," on her passage from Batavia to Rotterdam, struck upon one of the sunken rocks to the South West of Rosvear on the 21st of February, 1844. She was totally wrecked; and two only of the crew escaped. Their preservation was remarkable. They contrived to reach Rosevear. where they passed many hours in a state of fearful anxiety and suspense. The weather was very thick and hazy ; and their signals of distress were unnoticed. Providentially, on the following day they were discovered, and released from their dismal situation. It is but right to add, that their melancholy case awakened the sympathies of the Islanders, and elicited substantial acts of kindness, which the gratitude of the sufferers well repaid.

Close to Rosevear, towards the South, is Rosevean, and at some little distance South West, the Gilstone, on which Sir Cloudesley Shovel was wrecked on the 22nd of October, 1707. " Returning from Toulon in company with many other ships of war, in which were several distinguished personages, he came into soundings on the morning of the 22nd of October, 1707, and found his ship in nineteen fathoms of water. The weather at this time was thick and foggy, and the wind blowing strong ; which, with the supposition that they were nearing the land, induced him to make signal for the fleet to lay to. At six in the evening the admiral made sail again, and was followed by the rest of his fleet. This had scarcely been done before he hoisted signals of danger, which were repeated by several other ships, as a warning to those at a distance to keep off to sea. Sir George Byng, in the "Royal Anne," who was at this time about half a mile to windward of him, saw the breakers, and soon afterwards the rocks. His safety depended on the energies of a moment : for so near was his ship to a dangerous rock called the Tenemean, as to have it under his main chains, and as the ship passed, it knocked off the larboard quarter gallery, but happily he escaped without sustaining any further mischief.

E

"About eight o'clock at night, the admiral's ship, the 'Association,' struck upon the Gilstone with so much violence, that in about two minutes the vessel went down, and every soul on board, but one, perished. This man saved himself on a piece of timber, which floated to a rock called the Hellweathers, where he was compelled to remain some days before he could receive any assistance. Besides the 'Association,' the 'Eagle,' of 70 guns, Capt. Hancock, and the 'Romney,' of 50 guns, Capt. Cory, perished with all their crews. The 'Firebrand,' fire-ship was also lost, but Capt. Percy who commanded her, and most of his men were saved. The 'Phœnix,' fire-ship, Capt. Hansom, ran on shore, but was afterwards got off. The 'St. George,' commanded by Lord Dursley, seems to have escaped miraculously. She struck on the same rocks with the admiral, but the very same wave that beat out the lights of the 'Association,' lifted the 'St. George' from the rocks, and set her afloat again."

"Besides the admiral, there perished on this occasion, Capt. Lodes of the 'Association,' Sir John Narborough and his brother James, sons of Lady Shovel by a former husband ; Mr. Trelawney, eldest son to the Bishop of Winchester, and about 2000 men."†

From these dangerous Western rocks direct your course towards Annet. The isle to the East of Rosevean is Gorregan, and between the two, are high rocks called the Rags. Gorregan is a lofty islet, uncultivated, and about half a mile round. A single rock lies within Gorregan, named the Biggal of Gorregan. North East from Gorregan, is Meledgan,‡ and between this and Annet, are an almost countless multitude of rocks, which make the services of a trusty pilot absolutely necessary.

† Drew.

‡ At daylight on the 12th February, 1842, the top-gallant mast of a brig appeared above water, a little inside Gorregan. She proved to be the " William Proben," of South Shields, laden with wheat, and it is supposed that she struck on one of the Southernmost rocks. All the crew had perished, and no exact information could be gained on this subject.

Sailing by the reef of rocks called Hellweathers, and landing on the South East point of Annet, you should direct your steps towards the North Western extremity of the isle, called Annet Head. Here the rocks are of a fine, picturesque character, and form a prominent feature in the view from the other isles.

In the North East extremity of Annet is a chasm called Lake Anthown; it is about forty yards long, from three to four wide, and seven deep as far as has been traced, and has been supposed, without sufficient evidence, to have been an old iron mine. Annet is not inhabited. It contains about forty acres, which afford some tolerable pasturage for a few head of cattle. From this island you will gain a closer view of the Great Smith, a remarkably fine rock, lifting as it were its head out of the deep waters. It is especially bold on the Western side, and serves as a mark for different places, chiefly perhaps for the North West passage of the Broad Sound. The rock to the South East is the Little Smith.

From Annet the distance is but short across Smith's Sound to St. Agnes. You will land at Priglis Bay, so called from the Church near it.‡ Some writers have changed the name into Pericles Bay, and absurdly deduced from it an argument in support of the alleged Phœnician commerce with these Islands. In the fields behind this bay some urns or pots have been discovered in digging.

The origin of this Church deserves to be mentioned. In the year 1685, a French vessel struck upon the rocks, and the inhabitants of St. Agnes who repaired immediately to her assistance, having found her deserted, took possession, and with some exertion conducted her to St. Mary's. Here she was claimed by the captain, who, with the rest of his crew, had safely arrived thither in their boats. The islanders received a considerable sum for salvage, and being at that time without any place of worship, they agreed, with a unanimity that did honour to their piety, to appropriate the money to the building of a Church, which was

‡ See Note to Introductory Chapter.

accordingly done. The Church, so built, stood at the North West corner of the burial ground, and was replaced about forty years since by the present larger building.†

Keeping at the back of the Church and near the sea, you will be able to make your way with little difficulty round this part of the island. The rocks which form the cliff are very picturesque and beautiful. Different in character from most of the groups in Scilly, they shoot up into sharp points.

The high carn which next presents itself is Castle Bean ; and from it you will quickly reach St. Warna Bay, of which the legend is, that it derives its name from a saint who landed at this spot from Ireland. St. Warna was formerly invoked by the islanders as a benefactress in times of distress, sending wrecks and directing and presiding over other good fortune. St. Warna's Well is now filled up, lest, says Troutbeck, " the cattle or sheep should push one another into it when they came to drink," but its apparent size makes the statement doubtful.

Near this bay, upon somewhat higher ground, is a curious rock, called the Nag's Head. On this Southern side of St. Agnes occur in succession fine promontories of rock jutting out into the sea, and warm, sunny coves or bays. Each of these beautiful carns, which gird the island, has its particular designation : but it would be wearisome and useless to enquire names, forgotten as soon as heard. You must not fail, however, to see the Punch Bowl, a curious rock on the Wingletang Downs, to the South East of the Light-house. This rock has been supposed to be the Logan-stone on St. Agnes, described by Borlase in the following terms :—

" There is a very remarkable Stone of this kind on the Island of St. Agnes in Scilly. The under rock is ten foot six high, forty seven feet in circumference round the middle, and touches the ground with no more than half its base. The

† The visitor may with advantage proceed from the Church to the Light-house, (for a description of which see page 34) and afterwards resume the route pursued in the text.

upper Rock rests on one point only, so nice, that two or three men, with a Pole, can move it ; it is eight feet six high, and forty seven in girt. On the top is a large Basin, three feet eleven in diameter, (at a medium) at the brim wider, and three foot deep : by the globular shape of this upper Stone, I guess it has been rounded by art at least, if it was not placed on the hollow surface of the rock it rests upon by human force, which appears to me not unlikely."

The deep bay on the Southern side of St. Agnes, whose waters at spring tides mingle with those of the Western Ocean flowing into Perconger, over the bar of sand which separates the Gugh from the main land of St. Agnes, is called the Cove. It affords a most happy and convenient place for the islanders to obtain supplies of fish.

The inhabitants of the different Isles (with the exception of those on St. Martin's and Tresco, who draw their nets elsewhere) haul the cove, as the phrase is, in turn ; and it usually falls to the lot of each isle to haul twice in the course of the season. Not unfrequently a very large quantity of fish, between eighty and one hundred and forty baskets, is secured in a single night, each basket containing on an average, three hundred fish. The store, thus gathered from the deep, forms a main article of provisions for the winter.

Crossing the bar of sand the tourist should find time for a walk on the Gugh. It would seem that in Borlase's time this peninsula was never divided from St. Agnes, but by high and boisterous tides ; it is now always an island at spring tides, when there is a depth of water on the bar sufficient for a boat to shoot across it.

Sentinel at the North-West of the Gugh stands the Kittern, a fine picturesque rock, well worthy of notice. At the distance of about a quarter of a mile East by South of the Kittern is the Bow. The South Eastern point of land is called on the chart Dropnose Point, from a rock which bears that name at a small distance from the shore ; and near to this, Eastwards, is another with equal propriety called Wetnose.

There are several barrows upon the Gugh. At the North West extremity the visitor will see one between thirteen and fourteen feet long, four feet broad, and between two and three feet high. This lies on nearly the highest point of that part of the Gugh, just at the back, so to speak, of the Kittern.

Two more of these burial places may be discovered on the highest points of land towards the South East. They are not so large as the former ; nor have they so distinctly the marks of tombs, being nearly filled with soil and rubbish.

Still further in the same direction are two other barrows ; one in that heap of rocks which is called, for some uncertain reason, The Works. The other barrow lies on the high ground between The Works and the South West extremity of the Gugh. The latter is clearly seen from The Works and is not at a greater distance from them than fifty or sixty yards. This, the more Southern barrow, is between fourteen and fifteen feet in length, four feet six inches in breadth, and one foot six inches in depth. This barrow has four top or covering stones. Nearly in the centre of the Gugh is a pillar-stone. It is called by the islanders " the old man cutting turf " and is nine feet in length and seven feet in girth. Unlike the pillar-stones on St. Mary's, which stand quite erect, its inclination is so great that the top of it is not more than six feet and a half in perpendicular height from the ground. For whatever purpose it may have been originally placed, it is now used as a mark by the pilots for bringing vessels safely into the Road or Harbour, free of the Spanish ledges, a dangerous reef at the South Eastern entrance of St. Mary's Sound.

The Light-house requires a particular description. Its position was well chosen, so that it might serve not only as a beacon by night, but as a mark by day, and to aid this purpose, we shall find on approaching it that its walls are plastered of a dazzling whiteness. The Light-house was first built in 1680, by the Corporation of the Trinity House, and for more than a century the light was obtained

by means of a coal fire ; coals in large quantities were kept
burning near the top, and sometimes stirred with an iron
rod. According to Heath, the flame thus produced was
visible at a " vast distance upon the sea ; yet before the
coming of this present Light-keeper," he adds, " I've
known it scarcely perceivable in the night at the island of
St. Mary's, where it now looks like a comet. And some are
of opinion (not without reason) that in the time of the
former Light-keeper, it has been suffered to go out, or
sometimes not lighted."† Such a mode of lighting is
obviously rude and imperfect, even when carefully managed,
and in 1790, the Corporation provided the Light-house with
the present system of argand-lamps and reflectors. The
lamps, thirty in number, are symmetrically arranged on the
faces of a triangular prism which is made to revolve about
its axis once in three minutes, so that every point in the
horizon receives the full blaze of light once a minute ; the
revolution is effected by clock-work, which once wound up
will keep the machine in motion four hours. Each
lamp has a parabolic reflector at its back, made of
copper, lined with beaten silver. The lantern is about
twenty feet high, and its floor is about fifty feet from the
ground : outside it is a gallery used in cleaning its windows,
whence the visitor can command a magnificent view of all
the Islands, and if the weather be at all clear can also see
the distant coast of Cornwall. This prospect will well
repay the trouble of climbing to the lantern, whilst the
beautiful order and management within the Light-house
will probably excite admiration.

This excursion will have already occupied a summer's
day, but if the cove is to be hauled at dark, the visitor may
be induced to prolong his stay at St. Agnes till midnight.

† It was possibly in consequence of some report of these irregu-
larities that Whiston made his wonderful proposal to Parliament
in 1716, " that a ball of light or fire be thrown up from St. Mary's
every midnight and three times more every night, such as may
afford light above a degree of a great circle or sixty geographical
miles, and the sound heard above one third of that distance, both
of which we know from frequent experience may certainly be
done."

When the hour fixed for hauling has arrived, he should take up his position on the bar of sand crossed in visiting the Gugh. The net, which had been spread at the further extremity of the cove, is gradually drawn to the shore, and its contents will be deposited upon the sand. The scene is altogether striking. The multitude of fishes bouncing about on the ground, the dim lanterns moving here and there through the dark night,—for hauling takes place before moon-rise,—the lapping waters, and the splashing fish, concur to make this midnight excursion novel and interesting. The fish taken are principally scads ; though not unfrequently the haulers may be fortunate enough to get some red mullet, a salmon peel, or other choice fish.

FOURTH EXCURSION.

St. Martin's and the Eastern Islets.

Sailing from St. Mary's pier in a Northerly course the first point which invites attention is Carn Morval, forming the North East boundary of St. Mary's Pool or Harbour. We have referred to this fine bold mass of rocks in our Introductory Chapter ; and we must ask the reader to turn back to it, and reverse the course therein described through Crow Sound to the Eastern Isles.

The first appearance of this Eastern group is very pleasing. Borlase says " These Islets and Rocks edge this Sound in an extremely pretty, and very different manner from anything I had seen before. The sides of these little Islands continue their greenness to the brim of the water, where they are either surrounded by rocks of different shapes, which start up here and there as you advance, like so many enchanted castles, or by a verge of sand of the brightest colour. The sea, having eaten away passages between these hillocks, forms several pretty pools and lakes, and the crags which kept their stations, look so broken, intercepted, and so numerous, that the whole seemed but one large grotesque piece of rock-work."

F

The most convenient landing on Little Ganinick, the more Southerly of the two islets which lie to the Westward of this little archipelago is upon the Eastern side. This island, which contains between three and four acres, is at low water connected with Great Ganinick by a reef of rocks, so that you may easily pass from the one to the other ; but at high water there is between them a channel, seven feet, if not more, in depth. A suitable place for landing on Great Ganinick will be found at the North East end. There is not, however, except in the view which it offers of the adjoining islands, anything to repay the trouble. The area of Great Ganinick is about five acres and both isles are covered with long thick grass.

Great Arthur and Little Arthur contain from fifteen to twenty acres. These isles may be properly considered as one ; for it is only at high tides that the water washes over the stones which separate them, and at these times the waves flow also over the ridge of rocks which unites the Northern to the Southern extremity of Great Arthur : so that, in fact, this isle is at very high tides broken up into three islets. A bay of sand between Great and Little Arthur affords a convenient landing place.

Several barrows in more or less perfect condition, occur on Great Arthur. The best is on the Eastern hill, and is described by Woodley as consisting of a cromlech and sepulchral cave, in very good order. The walls of this cave are large flat stones, laid with their edges smooth ; and two very large stones are laid flat at the head of the grave, which appears to have been opened. It is about twelve feet long, four feet deep, and five feet and a half wide ; and is surrounded by an artificial mound, about forty yards in circumference.

There are also the ruins of two small houses, which were the temporary accomodations of parties who formerly resorted to this convenient place for the purpose of burning Kelp.

At the North East side of Little Arthur, is a large flat rock, called Arthur's Table.

On Little Ganilly, which comprises about six acres, the visitor may land at either end, according to the wind. Next to it is Ragged Island, so called from its very rough and uneven surface. It contains perhaps an acre and a half.

Great Ganilly looks well from the water. Its highest ground is about one hundred and seven feet above the sea, and it is the largest of these Eastern Isles, containing an area variously estimated from sixteen to twenty acres. The best place for landing is on the West side, towards the Southern end of it. From the higher points of land there is a very good view of the Seven Stones, which may be recognised by the line of white foam, caused by the breaking of the sea upon these rocks. The Reef so called lies somewhat less than three leagues from the Islands. It extends about one mile from North North West to South South East, and is perhaps the same distance in breadth. The two points of rock at the extremities of this dangerous reef, shewing themselves at half-tide only, are the Pollard to the North and the South Stone. In the Pollard two rings have been fixed, for the use of those who may wish to land upon the rock. There is very good fishing ground near these rocks much visited by the fishermen of Scilly.

The Light-ship was moored in August, 1841, about two miles to the East of the Seven Stones; and at present rides in very nearly the same position.

Menewethan lies to the South West of Great Ganilly; and those who can scramble may land on its Western side; but the best view, perhaps, of this fine mass of rocks is from the water. This island contains from four to five acres, and its highest point is eighty-seven feet above mean water.

To the North of Menewethan are Great and Little Inisvouls. The larger of these contains about two acres, the smaller, one; at low water both are united. Great Inisvouls is also connected with Great Ganilly by an isthmus of rock after the tide has ebbed for four hours.

Between these isles the inhabitants of St. Martin's and
of Tresco haul for their Winter stock of fish. They shoot
out five coils of line, each containing twenty fathoms, in
an Easterly direction towards Hanjague; and having
drawn the seine to the shore they "tuck up" the fish into
their boats, and return homewards, where they divide their
spoil.

Hanjague, which from its conical shape, is commonly
called the Sugar Loaf, is eighty-three feet in height, and the
water around it is twenty-five fathoms deep. A landing
can be effected only when the sea is quite calm, but it is
worth while to approach the rock for the sake of a closer
view.

The Mouls, between Inisvouls and Hanjague, always
presents three pointed rocks considerably above the surface
of the water; and is not, therefore, dangerous. Nornor
is also distinguished by three points of rock, of which the
Western is the highest; and contains about three acres.
The easiest place for landing is on the Southern side; but
in attempting to land on this or any other isle exposed to
the swell of the ocean, the side of the isle or rock most
sheltered from the wind should generally be chosen.

St. Martin's may be visited after Nornor. This island is
about two miles long, six miles round, and has an average
breadth of three quarters of a mile. St. Martin's formerly
suffered much from sands blown across it by the winds, and
hedges and other marks of enclosure and cultivation may
be traced in parts which are now abandoned to the sand.
From the same cause the island was gradually deserted, and
in the middle of the seventeenth century, it had not a single
inhabitant. Mr. Ekinis, the first steward that resided upon
the Islands under the Godolphin family, and the builder of
the Day-mark, to be presently described, encouraged a
re-settlement of St. Martin's, and it has now a population of
one hundred and eighty-five persons. The sandy soil is
pre-eminently favourable to the cultivation of potatoes; there
is a little good pasture, but as the ground is shallow and the
bottom rocky, the island suffers much from drought.

The inhabitants reside in three portions of the isle, severally called Higher, Middle, and Lower Town. Of these Higher Town is in every respect the most considerable. Its site is more eligible than that of the other two, as it is built on the high ground at the Southern extremity. The Church stands a little to the North of the principal houses, but as there is not a resident clergyman it can be opened for divine service only during the summer months; and then very occasionally.

On this, as on the three other principal islands, there is an Infant School, as well as one for the elder children.

The best landing place on St. Martin's is Perpitch Bay to the West of Carniweathers. A pleasant walk leads thence along the Eastern extremity of the isle to the Day-mark. This walk is the more inviting, from the distinct view which it affords of the pretty isles we have just described.

The fine, bold, precipitous mass of rock at the most Northerly point of the East end of St. Martin's is about one hundred and sixty feet in height. On the summit of this rocky headland is the Day-mark; which is somewhat above thirty feet high; and, from its position is visible at a distance of many leagues. The mark was built as we have said by Mr. Ekinis, and over the door are his initials T. E., with the date 1683. There is a stone staircase within leading to the top of the tower, whence there is a very extensive view in fine weather. During the last war a house was built near the Day-mark, for the use of the officer who had charge of the telegraph erected on this spot, but when peace was proclaimed it was to a great extent demolished by the islanders, either in the exuberance of their joy, or from the selfish motive of turning its materials to more profitable account.

This signal station was of considerable use during the great war. It is remembered that, on one occasion, a boat belonging to St. Mary's put off to a vessel, with the intention of offering some fresh fish for sale. She proved to be a French ship; and the English boat was soon sunk, and the crew made prisoners. Presently a signal was observed at St. Martin's head, which informed Captain Pellew that a French vessel was in sight. He immediately gave chase and brought her to action between the Isles and and the Lizard. After a very destructive engagement, the Frenchman was captured, and the islanders who had been sent below during the fight, were released. The ship was taken to Plymouth. In other instances, not a few, the communications made by the officer on duty at this station proved the means of safety to our merchantmen and ships of war.

Hanjague is due South East from the Day-mark. The two Chapel-rocks and Hardlewis-rocks lie East and East South East from the same point. They are not visible until half-tide.

Stretching to the West of St. Martin's Head is a deep bay, called Bread and Cheese Cove. The Eastern side of this cove is Chapel Brow; and the ridge of rocks running from the high ground to the sea is very bold and picturesque. Loop-hole Point is the name given by the islanders to the Western end of this cove; and the next bay is called Stony Porth. The promontory which forms the Western side of Stony Porth is Burnt Hill; a name probably derived from the appearance of the ground. The outer extremity of this headland is at high spring tides separated from the mainland of St. Martin's, and bears the name of Rat Island. Opposite Burnt Hill towards the North is a large rock, the Murr, so called, according to Woodley, from the sea-bird of that name by which it is frequented; but whatever may have been the case formerly, it is not now frequented by this or by any other sea-bird.

A little to the West is Culver Hole, which has been supposed to be an old tin-work. There is, however, no doubt but that it is a natural excavation; and the curious arch at the entrance of the hole or cavern, which will probably be swept away, ere long, by the encroaching tide, was formed by the falling away of the earth around it. At the distance of only a few yards to the West is another recess in the cliff of very similar appearance to Culver Hole.

The head-land' lying still more to the West is called
Turfy Hill.

Bull's Porth, above which are some fine rocks, is the name
given to the bay between Burnt Hill and Turfy Hill. The
rocks which lie off this part of the isle, at some little
distance in the sea, make it very dangerous to approach. To
the West North West of Murr Rock is Sandy's Ledge,
Mackerel Rock, and Merrick Ledge.

From Turfy Hill, the bay, which bears the name of the
island, stretches to the North West. It is half a mile in
length, and has a fine sandy shore. On the Eastern side of
it are three mounds of earth, of considerable size, which
are called the Frenchmen's Graves ; a name probably
derived from the wreck upon these rocks of some vessel
belonging to France. It is not unlikely, the bodies, of the
crew were deposited in those sands. Forming the Western
side of this bay, and nearly the extreme point to the North
of St. Martin's is a high carn, called Top Rock, which was
split with thunder on November 20th, 1751. So at least
says Troutbeck, who gives a full account of this disaster.

Due North of this Carn is White Island, to which the
visitor may pass on foot at low water. This isle contains
by estimation fifty acres,† and is chiefly remarkable for a
deep cavern situated nearly in the middle of its Eastern
side. Into this cavern it is possible to enter only at low
tides ; and those who have examined it, say you can penetrate twenty or thirty fathoms without reaching the end of
it. It is supposed to have been an old tin-work, its
direction is East and West. There is a rock on the surface
of the ground, which, in the opinion of some of the
islanders, marks the extreme distance to which you can go
under the ground.

Off the North Western end of St. Martin's and due
West of White Island is Pernagic Isle, which, as well as
Plumb Isle, lying to the South and nearer St. Martin's,
can be reached dry-shod, when the tide has ebbed two hours.

† Troutbeck, who is copied by Woodley.

At low tides it is possible to walk to Lion Rock, which is not far from Pernagic Isle.

On the dangerous brow of rocks which connects Lion Rock with Pernagic Isle, a vessel called the "Palinurus" was wrecked on the 27th of December, 1848. Seventeen bodies were recovered; and on the thirtieth, twelve were buried together in the church-yard of St. Mary's. Two were subsequently interred near the same spot; and the other three lie in the church-yard of St. Martin's. The vessel was bound from Demerara to England, and must, therefore, from some cause or other, have lost her proper course; but none survived to explain the deviation, or to tell who and how many had perished.

To the West South West of Lion Rock is Black Rock, between which and Round Island is the Channel for vessels sailing into Old Grimsby Harbour.

The name given by the islanders to the cove between Pernagic Point and Tinkler's Point, is Persile Bay. Tinkler's Point is nearly the most Western promontory of St. Martin's; and on it is a rock which bears the same name as the point. Near this are two circles of erect stones, (each circle about sixty feet in circumference,) and an ancient barrow. A visitor will have some difficulty in making out these circles, as some of the stones have been lately taken away for building houses near at hand.

To the South by West is a small hole in the cliff which gives its name to Goat's Point; and close to the shore, opposite the island of Tean, is a large heap of rocks, called Bab's Carn, from a family of that name, who lived close by it.

A pleasant walk leads hence along the good road recently made connecting the Eastern and Western extremities of the island.

The prospect from the South Eastern end of the road, in front of the houses, is very beautiful. The cultivated fields sloping towards the sea, present either from above or from below a pleasing appearance of fertility. Cruther's Bay, or, as it is marked in the map, Higher Town Bay, with its watch house, and the pilot boats riding at anchor in its calm waters ; Cruther's Hill on the right, stretching out into the sea and forming the South Western point of the Bay, which is bounded on the East by English Point Carn ; these several features in the scenery combined with the more distant objects, present a view of great interest and beauty.

The beach on the Western and Southern sides of St. Martin's has so very gradual a slope from the shore, that at low water it is not possible to reach the island even in small boats. This sand, called St. Martin's Flats, is one of the chief places in the Isles for the collectors of shells, especially towards its Southern end, between Guthers Isle and Higher Town.

ST. MARY'S.

Two days may easily be devoted to St. Mary's. It is the largest isle of the group, being about nine miles in circumference, and it exceeds in population all the other islands put together.

The island consists of two peninsulas of very unequal size connected by a low sandy isthmus, on which is built Hugh Town. The smaller peninsula is fortified, and called the Garrison, and the walk around it within the ramparts is very pleasing. The situation of Hugh Town, is, in many respects, bad ; the houses are so low that they are often flooded in Winter, when a storm happens at a spring-tide ; nor was it till the sixteenth century that it became the chief place in the island. Before that time Old Town was the principal village, but when the Garrison was fortified in the reign of Ellizabeth, Hugh Town naturally rose in importance. Its name is derived from Hugh, the former name of the small peninsula on which the Garrison is placed, which appears to signify " the high place," and to correspond to the Hoe so frequent in Devonshire. The houses in Hugh Town are for the most part small, but they are almost

universally furnished with neatness and comfort, and the
visitor is at once struck by the appearance of prosperity
among the inhabitants, which wider knowledge will show to
be borne out by reality. There are several shops of some
pretension, in which almost every article of domestic use
may generally be obtained. The main street leads from the
landward end of the pier past the Custom House, (built in
1841) along the sandy isthmus we have mentioned, and
then opens into a wider one called the Parade. Keeping to
the right hand of this, a road which passes by an Infant and
a National School on the left takes the visitor to the new
Church. The old church which we shall notice in the
perambulation of the island was about half-a-mile distant;
its grave-yard is still the place of burial of St. Mary's and
part of the church left standing is occasionally used as a
cemetery chapel. A tablet in the new church tells us that
it was erected in 1837, at the cost of King William IV.,
and was completed at the expense of Mr. Smith. It was
in fact begun when the King held the islands as Duke
of Cornwall, and finished by Mr. Smith after he became
the Lessee.

The visitor who has arrived at Scilly by the "Little
Western," and intends to remain only a few days cannot do
better than begin by an evening stroll around the Garrison
when he has refreshed himself after his voyage. In the
course of the walk he will see a succession of beautiful
prospects, rendered still more beautiful by the effects of the
setting sun, and he will at the same time get a clear
conception of the relative position of the several islands.

GARRISON.

The approach to it is by a somewhat steep hill rising to
a height of 110 feet above the level of the sea. Over the
entrance-gate hangs a large bell which is rung at certain
fixed hours of the day; and within the gate on the left
hand is the guard-room, containing the clock which
regulates the ringing of the bell, and an excellent

barometer placed there some years since by the then
inspecting commander Capt. Hall, R. N., for the especial
use of pilots and ship-masters. A broad walk leads from the
gate to the Star Castle, which stands on the highest ground
within the enclosure, and is so called from its star-like shape
due to its eight salient angles. The letters E. R. and the
date 1593, sculptured over the door, show the date of its
erection. Within are several semicircular rooms, in one of
which is a small but excellent library given by the associates
of the late Rev. Dr. Bray, for the use of the clergy
of the islands. The building of the Star Castle was a
consequence of the Spanish Armada, but little use was made
of it before the next century. In 1637, Dr. Bastwick was
confined there by the order of the Star Chambers for his
attacks on Episcopacy, and he remained immured in it, until
released by the Long Parliament. In 1646, Charles the
Second. then Prince of Wales, being obliged to quit
Pendennis Castle, landed in Scilly, on the 4th March ; and
lodged in Star Castle until the 17th April, when he sailed
for the Channel Islands, leaving Sir John Granville in
possession, the history of whose command will be found in a
subsequent chapter. From that time there was little to
distinguish Star Castle, until the month of September, 1846,
when the Queen, the late Prince Albert, the Prince of
Wales, and the Princess Royal, visited it in the course of a
voyage around the Western coast.

From Star Castle, the road along the North side of the
Garrison enclosure may be followed. The view looking
North takes in the whole of the pool and roads, bounded
by St. Martin's on the North East, Tresco and Bryher, on
the North, and a little to the left of the last appear the two
conical hills of Sampson. Within the Garrison itself a
battery named Jefferson's, is seen to the North East,
furnished with one nine-pounder, and two six-pounder guns,
and three eighteen-pounder carronades, whilst near it, on
the left, is the Master Gunner's Battery, with three
eighteen-pounder carronades, protecting the Master
Gunner's House. Continuing the walk the bomb-proof

store-house is passed, and the store-house battery with three
thirty-two pounders and one eighteen pounder, looking
N. W. by N.; and still further on, the entrance
to the Road is protected by Charles's Battery, with
two thirty-two-pounders fronting N. W. It is
impossible to take this walk on a Summer evening without
starting innumerable rabbits, which scamper across the
paths in all directions. A few years since Mr. Smith
placed some deer in the enclosure, but he did not succeed in
rearing any.

The most westerly point of the Garrison is called the
Steval, from a rock of the same name just opposite to it.
An eighteen pounder is placed here. The point
commands a good view of the Bishop Light House in the
extreme South West. The next battery is Bartholomew's,
armed with three eighteen pounders ; it is immediately
opposite St. Agnes, the Light House of which is of course
distinctly visible. A Summer sunset seen from this part of
the walk is often a spectacle of great beauty, and the visitor
who is fortunate enough to enjoy it will probably be not
ungrateful to Mr. Smith for the benches placed judiciously
here and there along the promenade.

At the Woolpack Battery, opposite the Woolpack rock,
and facing South, are four, thirty-two-pounder, and four,
eighteen-pounder guns, one eighteen-pounder being on a
wooden carriage, and pointed at the salient angle. From
the interior of this battery there is a good view of the pretty
Carn which stands at this Southern point of the garrison.
The Batteries which follow this are the Morning Point (five
thirty-two pounders), and Bentam's (one eighteen pounder
and one nine pounder). The view at these points takes in
the open sea at the south, and the little bay of Porcrasa,
bounded on the opposite side by the rocks of Peninis, and
when the Duke of Leed's Battery with its three eighteen-
pounder carronades is reached, the visitor looks down on
the houses of Hugh Town. A little further on, King
George's Battery of four eighteen pounder carronades, close
to the gate marks the end of the circuit.

We have described this walk as seen on a Summer's evening, but its beauty is not less striking, though of a different order during a Wintry gale. The little peninsula everywhere bounded by a rocky shore is then encircled on the leeward side by a ring of furious foam, whilst on the windward the waves are continually rising and breaking on the rocks. Huge waves course through the roads, and the outlying islands are partially hidden by sheets of foam. The mildness of the climate allows the most delicate persons to venture out and enjoy the spectacle without experiencing any greater inconvenience than that of having to face the force of the wind ; and the spectator safe on land may often feel the proverbial pleasure of watching a stout vessel labouring with the gale.

PENINIS, &c.

The rocks at Peninis (the Head of the Island) are the boldest and finest to be seen in Scilly, and their fantastic shapes afford the best examples of the disintegration for which the granite of the islands is remarkable. There are two ways of reaching Peninis, but whichever route be chosen the visitor must first proceed towards Porerasa, a fine bay on the Southern side of the island, extending from the Garrison to Buzza Hill. From Porerasa he may pursue a foot-path, through the fields skirting the bay on the left, which leads directly to the head-land or by following another path which tends in a South Easterly direction from the end of Buzza Street, he may ascend Buzza Hill, recognizable by its windmill, and proceed thence to the point. The view from the summit is extensive, and the hill itself with its masses of grey stone protruding between ferns and furze bushes is not wanting in picturesqueness. Three barrows are said to have once existed on this hill, but only one to the South West of the wind mill is now discoverable ; the others were not improbably destroyed, to furnish material for the mill, or for some similar purpose.

These, who has made the circuit of the Garrison, will be able to name most of the objects seen from Buzza Hill. The panorama is the same regarded from a different point of view ; to the North are Hugh Town, the Pool, Sampson, Bryher and Tresco, and a little to the West of South, St. Agnes with its Lighthouse ; but ascending the sloping ground which lies towards the South, a new and commanding view of Peninis is obtained, and midway between this station and the headland, lies a carn called the Dutchman's carn which deserves notice. Proceeding from this carn to the point, a remarkable group of rocks on some upper ground is first reached. They are called the Kettle and Pans from the deep and beautifully curved rock-basins found on them, which were long supposed to have been used in, if not made for, the rites of Druidical worship. Dr. Borlase who published in 1756, a short narrative of a visit to Scilly, gives a long description of these basins which it is not necessary to quote. He indulged in very fanciful suggestions as to their use, and called attention to the fact, that at a little distance from them, " there shoots up a pro-digious rock, thin, pyramidal, twelve feet at the base, and thirty feet high, not improbably an object of the Druid Devotion." Both the basins and the thin pyramidal rock are however the effect of the same natural action which has produced the other fantastic forms of Peninis, nor is there a tittle of evidence that any of them were ever used in Druidical worship. In the paper read before the Royal Geological Society of Cornwall, by the late Mr. Joseph Carne, F. R. S., printed in the appendix to this volume, will be found an excellent description of the action of decomposition and disintegration ; but a short summary of it may not be out of place here. The granite of Scilly is remarkable for its jointed structure ; the rocks are intersected by lines which in fact correspond to these planes and are generally reducible to one of three systems ; they are either horizontal, or vertical, and North and South, or vertical and East and West. At these joints the action of decomposition is easy, and the blocks of granite are changed by it into the form of cheeses or columns, according as the

planes are horizontal or vertical. In the formation of rock
basins the granite is actually disentegrated or worn to its
elements, instead of being separated into masses ; this process is most actively carried on where the granite is most
exposed to wind and rain. At Peninis decomposition and
disintegration may be seen in all its stages, cracks extending
vertically, and masses separating into horizontal layers, are
constantly met with, and rock-basins occur in the first form
of a mere finger-mark, then as a perfect spherical hollow,
sometimes five or six feet in diameter, and three feet deep,
and then a lip is broken and the basin becomes after a time
an easy chair or a couch end. At the bottom of the basin
a little rain water will generally be found continuing the
work of destruction, and in the basin grains of quartz and
felspar, which has been freed from the granite. From the
Kettle and Pans, the visitor may proceed to the extremity
of the head-land. He must however be prepared for a
scramble and must take care that the tide does not intercept
his return. On the way the pyramidal rock mentioned by
Dr. Borlase, called the Tooth Rock will be easily recognized.
The peculiar rock on the top of the head-land bearing the
appropriate name of the Monk's Cowl, may be reached with
a little difficulty. It is one hundred and four feet, seven
inches above the mean level of the sea.

Returning from the point the way may be retraced to
Pitt's Parlour just under the Tooth Rock. The explanation usually given of this name is, that in days long since
gone by, a party of friends, of whom a Mr. Pitt was one,
were wont to spend their Summer evenings together in this
retired and romantic spot.

From this height, may be commanded a fine view of the
Southern ocean, when lashed into fury by a storm. If the
wind has prevailed for some time from the South or the
South West, the waves break very grandly at the base of
the rocks, the sheets of spray dash over the masses of
granite which await their onset, and with a deafening roar
the tide rushes up the narrow ravine or channel which, in
he lapse of ages, the waters have hollowed for themselves.

It is scarcely necessary to direct a visitor's attention to the large masses of rock before, above, and on either side of him. The semicircle of high, bold rocks, which is crowned by the Monk's Cowl, presents a grand appearance from Pitt's Parlour ; and fine blocks of granite, of every shape and size, are scattered in all directions around. By going to the other side of the ravine which lies beneath and opposite to the Parlour, a different and not less imposing view of the promontory will be obtained. Here, too, imbedded among huge piles of rock, is Sleep's abode, (called also a parlour.) It is both difficult of approach and hard to be found ; but the trouble of searching it out is well rewarded by a sight of the vast masses of rock which are there heaped together.

From Peninis around the cliffs in an Easterly direction, a path towards Old Town may be followed, in the course of which several rocks of curious shapes and various dimensions will be passed. On the right is a far-extending and irregular field of rock, for almost every part of which the islanders have a particular name. Here is the Jolly Rock, marked in the map, which is often visited by fishing parties ; and here too, in the cliff, is Piper's Hole, at the distance of fifteen or twenty feet below the turf trod by the pedestrian. The latter is, however, a wretched little cave, and is not worth the fatigue and trouble of search, unless it be for the purpose of obtaining a draught from the clear spring of fresh water which is certainly found within it.

From Piper's Hole the distance is but short to the Pulpit Rock, a remarkable specimen of the effect of horizontal decomposition. It is difficult to conceive a rock more curiously perched than that which bears this appropriate name. It consists of a flat rock forty-seven feet in length, and twelve feet in (mean) breadth, branching out from a short thick rock as from a pillar. It projects horizontally over a smaller rock, which might well serve as a pulpit to one, who, with a voice louder than that of Stentor, would essay to address in language of exhortation or command the captains of a fleet assembled on the waters beneath him. The flat rock above his head would worthily supply the place of a sounding board ; and if it were possible to conceive the voice of man reaching from this point to sailors on the deep below, the pulpit and the sounding board would be in good keeping with the grandeur and sublimity of the scene. It is easy to mount to the top of the sounding board ; and thus to form a more correct opinion of the length and breadth of this curious rock, which is one of the most conspicuous features in the scenery of the coast. The view on all sides is exceedingly fine. Immediately towards the sea are vast masses of rock, very many tons in weight ; at a short distance from the shore is a solitary mass of granite called Carrickstarne, (the Saddle Rock) ; and on the Eastern side of the Bay, a bold, rocky cliff stretching towards the main-land. Nor are the other features in the scene less calculated to draw attention. Carn Lea, the extreme point of Old Town Bay, to the West, the Bay itself with its sandy beach, the remains of the old Church and the grave-stones around it, the cluster of cottages in Old Town and the green fields, and meadows, varying the prospect and relieving the eye, will all claim some share of notice and remark.

It is possible to reach Old Town by a nearly direct route, passing close to Carn Lea, but it will be necessary to force a way over rocks and rough hedges of stones. An easier course is the path which leads to the Tower, standing about two hundred yards from Pulpit Rock. This Tower was chosen by a party of the Sappers and Miners under the direction of Sergeant Steel, as the spot from which to make their trigonometrical observations. Its height above mean water was determined by them to be one hundred and forty one feet. From this tower a narrow road leads towards Hugh Town ; by following it to the point where it meets the main road, and then turning towards Old Town, the Church-yard and remains of the old church will be reached.

Only a small portion of the old Church, as before observed, is standing. It was built in the form of a cross; though at what period is uncertain. It appears from Troutbeck's narrative to have been enlarged in 1662, by the addition

of a North aisle; and from a memorandum in the earliest
of the parish register books, we learn "that the Southern
aisle of the Church of Saint Mary's, in Scilly, was begun to
be built on the sixth day of June, 1677."+ The length of
the church from East to West, was sixty feet, and the
breadth of the nave nineteen feet; the length from end to
end of the transepts was sixty-two feet, and their
breadth sixteen feet. The Church had greatly
fallen into decay, partly through age, yet more
through neglect, when the building of the new Church in a
situation more accessible to the inhabitants of Hugh Town,
was determined upon by King William IV. The bodies of
Henry Trelawny, son of Sir Jonathan, the famous Bishop,
Sir John Narborough, and Captain Lodes, all of whom
perished with Sir Cloudesley Shovel, were buried in the
chancel.

The Church-yard is still used and is neatly kept. A
monument of black marble on the outside of the East end
of the Church deserves notice. It is dedicated to the
memory of Frances, the wife of Joseph Hunkin, the
Governor of the Islands under the Commonwealth, and
bears the arms of the husband and wife. It was originally
placed within the Church, and after having been shifted from
its first position when the South aisle was built, was again
taken down, and for some time remained in pieces in a
corner. The families of both husband and wife were found on
enquiry to be extinct, but "I thought it a pity" writes the
gentle Troutbeck "that such an ancient monument which must
have cost a considerable sum, should be concealed in such
a manner, so I interceded with the late churchwardens to
have it put up in the wall of the church, on the outside of
the East end, where it may be seen by all curious people."
A tablet to the memory of John, the son of Thomas Ekines,
with the motto "non mortuus sed dormit," may interest
those who have visited St. Martin's, and seen the Day-mark,
the monument of Thomas Ekines' public spirit. In the

+ In the same register is the following entry. Scilly, November
21st, 1742. Bryber Chapel was dedicated to the pious memory of All
Saints, by me, Paul Hathaway, minister to the Islands of Scilly.

South East corner of the church-yard close to the wall is an upright slate to the memory of Abraham Leggatt, a surgeon; the singular position of this stone was according to tradition chosen that it might face the cottage of a maiden of Old Town, of whom Leggatt was passionately fond. Truth however compels us to add that the enamoured surgeon had a wife of his own at the time.

The parsonage formerly stood next the church-yard, close to the road at the head of Old Town Bay. In this bay the conger fishery was formerly carried on to a great extent. A stone trough, now a support to a shed attached to one of the houses, was formerly used for salting fish in, and it is said that all the fish from every island, were brought hither to be cured, when stages were erected in a field adjoining, for drying them in the sun. The trough is of one stone, holds eighteen Winchester bushels, and was dug from a quarry upon Sallakee Downs, about half a mile distant. Large supplies of the fish so cured were carried up the Straits, and exported to other places. This was an extensive branch of trade, and of great advantage to the Isles, until it was superseded by the pilchard fisheries of Mount's Bay.

The Eastern extremity of Old Town Bay, is called Tolmen Point. The name is derived from a rock upon it called the Tolmen, *i. e.* rock-table, and not holed rock as supposed by Dr. Borlase. An absurd story about monks levying toll is an ignorant invention of a late period.

Near the Tolmen is a sod battery, where three guns formerly stood. Two of them were taken away about a century ago, and the third has been removed upwards of forty years.

In the bay, about midway between Carn Lea and the Tolmen point, is the Gull Rock, and further South is the Gilstone. These rocks must have always made Old Town Bay dangerous, yet it is clear that Old Town was once the principal place in St. Mary's, and this the principal anchorage. The Church lay to the West, and the Castle stood on the high ground to the North East, scarcely less than one hundred feet above the level of the sea. Some remains of the Northern wall may still be traced. It is impossible now to ascertain the early history of this Castle, but it is probably the same as the Castle of Ennor in Scilly, described in 1306, as held of the King by the service of finding and maintaining ten armed men to keep the peace. When Leland visited the Islands about 1540, it was in adequate repair, but upon the building of Star Castle it became neglected, if it was not already ruined, and its walls served as a quarry to the neighbouring cottagers.

At a short distance from Old Town, towards the North East, is one of the best gardens in the island. The myrtle hedges, mesembryanthemums, and other plants rarely found, except in greenhouses, on the main land, which are growing here in great beauty, give good proof of the advantages of climate enjoyed in the Islands, and show that floriculture may be carried to any extent, if only the hurtful effects of storm and wind can be prevented by seasonable shelter. Dr. Borlase has made the same observation. " Roots of all kinds, Pulse and Sallets grow well ; Dwarf Fruit-trees, Gooseberries, Currants, Raspberries, all Shrubs, and whatever rises not above their hedges do very well ; and even these would do better, if they would provide against storms, by planting shelters of Elder, Dutch elm, Sycamore, and the like, in Clumps and Hedge-rows; and 'till they can reconcile themselves to the trouble and time of raising such shelters, all their Vegetables must be exposed, in proportion to their height, to the winds ; but to tell you the truth, the true spirit of planting either has never reached here, or has been forced to give way to more necessary calls." Dr. Borlase, published his letter in 1756, and his remarks may have induced three inhabitants of Scilly (J. B., S. M., M. C.,) to write to the *Gentleman's Magazine*, in April, 1757, to enquire what trees would grow near the sea. Mr. Urban, recommended sycamore, sallow thorn, fir and poplars, and it is possible that the trees at Holy Vale, to be presently mentioned, owe their existence to this correspondence.

Parting, or Parton Carn, lies a little past the garden which
has caused this digression, and a quarter of a mile further
on the right hand is Tremelethen.   The gardens and
orchards belonging to this farm show the produce of the
island.   It consists, chiefly, of a great variety of apples,
and the trees at Tremelethen have the advantage of a
warm aspect and good shelter.

Continuing the walk along the road a view is gained of
the comfortable farm at Longstone, rejoicing in the warmth
of a Southern sky ; but, before reaching it, the road
changes its direction and bears towards the farms at
Carnifriers, so called from Carn Friars, a small heap of
rocks lying near.   It is possible that Carn Friars and the
neighbouring Holy Vale, point to some Chapel and
Cell of the Tresco foundation, but we know of no other
warrant than the names for the supposition.

Leaving these farms on the right, a way should be taken
over a gently sloping field which lies nearly North East.
At the farther corner of this field is a rough road to a farm
called Normandy, towards the Eastern extremity of
St. Mary's.   Thence Northward, across a common and
along a road, a succession of pretty views will be presented,
until Maypole, the hill above Holy Vale, is reached.   This
hill affords one of the prettiest prospects on St. Mary's.
At its foot is Holy Vale, a pleasant sheltered nook, with
four good substantial farm houses.   This farm for about
two centuries belonged to a family of the name of Crudge,
the last member of which died in November, 1848, at the
advanced age of ninety-seven.   The first of the family who
came to Scilly was Mr. John Crudge, of Tolver, in the
parish of Gulval, near Penzance, who married Ursula,
second daughter of Sir Francis Godolphin, then lessee of the
Islands.   The pair settled in Scilly, and their descendants
remained there enjoying some honour on account of their
connection with the Godolphin family ; the post of
Commissary of the Musters seems to have been hereditary
amongst them.   This central farm has a warm aspect,
it looks towards a little Southern Cove, called Porth

Hellick, and is well sheltered from the North winds, as the trees growing about it show. One of the finest trees, a sycamore, is said to have been cut down, to make room for the house which now stands at right angles to the principal building. The original farm, or, more correctly, the farm which was built after the first was destroyed by fire, consisted of the two central houses. The neat gardens in Holy Vale, in which there are some choice myrtles and a fine aloe, deserve notice.

The road, for a short distance, is shaded by trees, which, screened from the violence of the winds, are of a less stunted growth than elsewhere in the Islands. As soon as their ·friendly shelter is passed, a stile upon the left hand points to a foot-path which winds in a pretty circuit towards the South. By taking this path a view of the orchards and gardens belonging to Holy Vale is obtained, and the high ground above Longstone is reached.

From this elevation there is a nearer view of the fresh water at Porth Hellick and of the inland scenery of St. Mary's. The path above the farm leads to the new road, nearly at the point which bears towards Tremelethen. This well-made road was planned some fifteen years since by Mr. Smith, and was executed by a sort of corvée under his direction. It is one of the benefits due to his good government, of which we shall have more to say in the chapter on the social condition of the Islands.

SIXTH EXCURSION.

THE NORTH COAST OF ST. MARY'S.

In our Sixth excursion we purpose to traverse the North and East coast of St. Mary's, starting from Hugh Town, and going round as far as Old Town, the limit of the fifth excursion. By this means we shall make a complete circuit of the island.

The first point of interest is Carn Thomas, a bold point of land projecting about one hundred yards into St. Mary's Pool, and dividing it into two beautiful bays. The height of the topmost rock of the carn is eighty feet above the level of the sea, and the visitor who ascends it may find himself tempted to rest and lounge away a summer morning, watching the small occupations of the harbour. The little bay or cove to the East of this Carn is Permellin; its beach is covered by a remarkably fine sand, parcels of which were sent in Heath's time as presents to Cornwall, and more distant parts of England, to be used in drying ink, and for scouring brass, pewter, &c. The sand of Permellin is, however, specially remarkable for the thin ridges of black mica, which lie in streaks over the fine quartz which forms the bulk of it; the mica lies parallel to the line of the advancing waves, and seems as if deposited by successive tides : scarcely any is found below the surface. The white sand marked with these faint black lines presents a beautiful appearance, but the explanation of the phenomena is not very clear ; it is probable that the mica is a residuum of the decomposition of the granite of Carn Thomas, and in Mr. Carne's paper in the appendix will be found an hypothesis on the subject.

On the hill above Permellin to the East, called Mount Flagin, or Flagon, are the few remains of Harry's walls. Amongst the fortifications of the coast projected in the early part of the reign of Henry VIII., was a fort on this spot ; the situation was ill chosen, and either on this account, or for the more probable reason, want of money, the work was, like so many others, abandoned at an early stage.

There is a curtain, with two bastions, remaining ; the latter are hollow, and project with very acute angles. The length of the whole is sixty-two yards; the face of each bastion sixteen yards ; the walls are from ten to twelve feet thick, and about five feet high. Such was the peculiar excellence of the cement used in this work, that but few of the stones have been dislodged notwithstanding the exertions that have been made for that purpose; and the fortress may probably remain in its present state for centuries to come.

On the North side of these walls, and on the summit of the hill, is an upright stone or menhir. It is placed in a most commanding position, and stands about nine feet and a half above the ground. Proceeding along the coast we pass two islands, the more Northerly of which is called Taylor's Island, the other Newford. The former at high water appears a pretty carn rising out of the sea. Mr. Carne has remarked that in the granite of Taylor's Island, the mica has been replaced by minute prisms of tourmaline, often with a perfect termination.

1

The Bay nearly opposite Taylor's Island, is Porthloo,. flanked on the North East by Carn Morval. The view at this latter point is one of the finest the Islands afford, but it is surpassed in extent by that seen from the top of Telegraph Hill. To reach this hill, the visitor must strike inland by a path across some fields covered with golden furze. From the top of the Telegraph, which is two hundred and four feet above mean water, the principal. objects in St. Mary's, and the relative situation of the other isles, are visible. In the distance, the Eastern group, St. Martin's, Tean, Menavawr, Tresco, with the harbours of Old and New Grimsby on either side, Bryher, the two hills of Sampson, the Broad Sound, Annet, St. Agnes, and the far stretching isles and rocks to the West : in the foreground, the farms and downs of St. Mary's.

Nearly due North from the Telegraph, is Bant's Carn, and according to Troutbeck, a small village named Bant's farm was situated near it. To the South West of this carn is a barrow in very good preservation. It has three top or covering stones; and its sides are secured by flat stones in the ordinary manner. It is about twelve feet in length, three feet six inches wide, two feet six inches in height. On the downs, to the East South East of this, there is another barrow from which the top stones have been removed. It is otherwise very complete.

In the immediate neighbourhood of the Telegraph, are two or three small farms, one of which, Newford, may be specified, as the date of the plantation of the orchard attached to it is known. It was planted in 1750, by Mr. Thomas Smith, then steward to the Earl of Godolphin.

About a quarter of a mile to the North West of Newford, and the same distance to the North East of the Telegraph is another menhir, called by the inhabitants the Long Rock; it is nearly nine feet high, and ten feet round the thickest part. From the Long Rock the visitor may walk to the North East and reach the sea at Inisidgen Point, which is in fact the North Eastern extremity of St. Mary's. This point derives its name from the island of Inisidgen (in.

'Borlase Enys-an-geon, St. John's Island?) immediately
opposite to it. The carn on the point is well worthy of
examination, and its proximity to the Eastern islands and
St. Mary's secures a very pretty view. But that which
makes this hill an object of especial interest is a remarkably
fine barrow on nearly its highest point. It is very large
and in excellent preservation. Its dimensions are about
fourteen feet in length, four feet six inches in width, and
three feet eight inches in height; and it has five top or
covering stones.

From Inisidgen Point the coast turns in a Southerly direction to Watermill Bay. A little stream running into this
cove may serve to explain its name, though the " mill " has
long since disappeared. The stream is supplied by the fine
spring called Lentevern Well, which seems to have been
formerly known also as Carnidgen Well, the connection
between which and Inisidgen is evident. A pleasant
walk along 'the cliff leads to New Quay, and thence
to Toll's Island, and Mount Todden. At the last
named 'place is a battery called Pellew's redoubt, from the
signal gun, an eighteen pounder, which Lord Exmouth
placed there when in command of this station. There is
a small watch-house close by, in which, during the wars of
the last century, a soldier of the garrison and three islanders
kept watch every night against surprise from privateers of
the enemy.

Leaving Mount Todden, Deep Point, the most Easterly
point of the island is soon reached. The rocks hereabout are
very fine, and exhibit in great perfection the several processes
of disintegration and decomposition. Normandy Gap is
perhaps second only to the rocks at Peninis. Other rocks
worthy of notice are the Sun Rock and the Clapper Rocks ;
and Mr. Carne noticed a rock about a quarter of a mile
North of the Sun Rock, where a large block of granite
rests upon another block, the space between the two being no
more than a few inches, whilst on the surface of the lower
are three regular basins, which could in no case have been
worked out by tools. Rock basins are found on all the

rocks in this neighbourhood, and their number and position are constantly undergoing a change. Not far from the Clapper Rocks is Dick's Carn, near which are several barrows very similar in form and dimensions to those already noticed, but all of them appear to have been opened.

Continuing our perambulation we arrive at Porth Hellick, (cove of willows) on the beach of which Sir Cloudesley Shovel found a burial until his body was taken up and removed to Westminister Abbey.† We have described (p. 29,) the circumstances of his shipwreck ; his body was carried by the tidal current to the South of the Islands and washed ashore at Porth Hellick. Former historians of Scilly have, with a ridiculous prudery, suppressed the popular belief in Scilly about the Admiral. There is no reason whatever for crediting it with a foundation in fact, but the picturesqueness of the tradition gives it a claim to be preserved. The story runs that a common sailor on board the Admiral's vessel warned the officer of the watch that their course was bearing on the rocks of Scilly, and this being reported to Sir Cloudesley incensed him against the man. The sailor was summoned aft, and persisting in his opinion was ordered to be hanged at the yard-arm for disobedience, and exciting a spirit of mutiny. He requested permission to read a psalm aloud before his execution, and the request being granted he selected the sixty-ninth, the curses of which may be remembered. Nothing daunted at the threats thus thrown at him, the Admiral hanged the man, and early the same night his vessel was shipwrecked. The tradition goes on that the Admiral escaped drowning, and was washed ashore alive though almost exhausted, and that an islander who found him, and at first was solicitous to assist him, was struck with such a covetous desire for a valuable ring worn on his finger, that for the sake of it he put him to death. Sir Cloudesley was buried on the beach,

† Addison, who must have known Sir Cloudesley,(he was Under-Secretary of State at the time of the shipwreck) has justly ridiculed the representation of him on the tomb in the Abbey, as a beau in a long periwig.

and as a further sign of God's wrath at his injustice and
violence, the grass has never since grown on the spot where
he was laid. The last circumstance admits of an easy
rationalistic explanation ; the sand of the beach is covered
with a thin growth of grass, having little or no root, and
wherever the grass is once disturbed it will not grow again
for many years. Many of the islanders hold, however, to
the supernatural refusal of the grass to grow, and the place
of Sir Cloudesley's grave is still pointed ont by them.

To the North of Porth Hellick beach, is a large pool of
fresh water, which abounds with eels, mullets, and flounders.
Nearly due West of this pool, is a farm house called
Sallakey, which gives their names to the fields forming the
high ground towards the South.

Dr. Borlase, in his "Antiquities," describes a plane of rock
one hundred and seventy-two feet from North to South,
and one hundred and thirty-eight from East to West,
situate near Sallakey. " We found " he writes " the back
of the rock cleaved by art (at least so it seemed to us) of
all unevenness," but those who may visit it now, will see
that in little more than a hundred years the surface has
become covered with small basins, drains, and shallow
excavations.

On Sallakey Hill are two stone crosses of the oldest and
rudest construction. They are now fixed in the stone
hedge : one to the East at the Northern corner of the field ;
the other to the West in the middle of the wall near a gate.
Neither has any inscription, nor any figure discernable,
and both are of inconsiderable size.

Porth Hellick is associated with an escape from shipwreck
more authentic than the tale of Sir Cloudesley Shovel, and
even more marvellous. The narrative which we transcribe
was first printed in Mr. Courtney's "Guide to Penzance,"
(1845), and as it was furnished to him by the late Richard
Pearce, Esq., French Consular Agent at Penzance, there
can be no doubt of its correctness.

" The brig ' Nerina,' of Dunkerque, sailed from that
place on Saturday, the 31st of October, 1840, under the

command of Capt. PIERRE EVERAERT, with a cargo of oil and canvass for Marseilles : her burthen was about one hundred and fourteen tons ; the crew consisted of seven persons, including the captain and his nephew, a boy fourteen years old.

" At three o'clock in the afternoon of Monday, the 16th of November, they were forced to heave-to in a gale of wind, at about ten or twelve leagues South West of the Scilly Islands. At seven o'clock of the same evening, still lying-to under their close reefed main-top-sail, and balanced reefed main-sail, a heavy sea struck the vessel and she suddenly capsized, *turning completely bottom up.*

" The only man on the deck at the time was named BOUMELARD, who was instantly engulfed in the ocean. In the forecastle were three seamen—VINCENT, VANTAURE, and JEAN MARIE : the two former, by seizing hold of the windlass-bits succeeded in getting up close to the keelson, and so kept their heads above water. Poor JEAN MARIE was not so fortunate,—he must have been in some measure entangled ; as, after convulsively grasping the heel of VANTAURE for a few seconds, he let go his hold and was drowned. His body was never seen afterwards. The other two, finding that the shock of the upset had started the bulkhead between the forecastle and the hold, and that the cargo itself had *fallen down on the deck*, contrived to draw themselves on their faces close alongside the keelson, (for it could not be called on their hands and knees for want of height) towards the stern of the ship, from whence they thought they heard some voices.

" At the time of the accident, the captain, the mate JEAN GALLO, and the boy NICHOLAS NISSEN, were in the cabin. The captain caught the boy in his arms, under the full impression that their last moments had arrived.

" The mate succeeded in wrenching open the trap-hatch in the cabin deck, and in clearing out some casks which were jammed in the lazarette (a sort of small triangular space between the cabin floor and the keelson, where stores are generally stowed away) : having effected this, he scrambled up into the vacant space and took the boy from the hands of the captain, whom he then assisted to follow them.

" In about an hour they were joined by VINCENT and VANTAURE from the forecastle. There were then five individuals closely cooped together : as they sat they were obliged to bend their bodies for want of height above them, whilst the water reached as high as their waists : from which irksome position one at a time obtained some relief by stretching at full length on the barrels in the hold, squeezing himself up close to the keelson.

" They were able to distinguish between day and night by the light striking from above into the sea, and being reflected up through the cabin sky-light, and then into the lazarette through the trap-hatch in the cabin floor.

" The day and night of Tuesday, the 17th, and day of Wednesday, the 18th, passed without food, without relief, and almost without hope ; but still each encouraged the others, when neither could hold out hope to himself,— endeavouring to assuage the pangs of hunger by chewing the bark stripped off from the hoops of the casks. Want of fresh air threatening them with death by suffocation, the mate worked almost incessantly for two days and one night in endeavouring, with his knife, to cut a hole through the hull. Happily the knife broke before he had succeded in accomplishing his object, the result of which must have proved fatal, as the confined air alone preserved the vessel in a sufficiently buoyant state.

" In the dead of the night of Wednesday, the 18th, the vessel suddenly struck heavily : on the third blow the stern dropped so much that all hands were forced to make the best of their way, one by one, further towards the bows ; in attempting which poor VINCENT was caught by the water and drowned, falling down through the cabin floor and sky-light.

" After the lapse of an hour or two, finding the water to ebb, GALLO got down into the cabin, and whilst seeking for the hatchet, which was usually kept there, was forced to

rush again for shelter to the lazarette, to avoid being
drowned by the sea, which rose on him with fearful
rapidity. Another hour or two of long suffering succeeded,
when they were rejoiced to see by the dawning of the day
of Thursday, the 19th, that the vessel was fast on rocks,
one of which projected up through the sky-light. The
captain then went down into the cabin, and found that the
quarter of the ship was stoved ; and looking through the
opening, he called out to his companions above, ' Grace à
Dieu mes enfans, nous sommes sauves ! je vois un homme à
terre !' (Thank God, my children, we are saved ! I see
a man on the beach !) Immediately after this the man
approached and put in his hand, which the captain seized,
almost as much to the terror of the poor man as to the
intense delight of the captain. Several people of the
neighbourhood were soon assembled ; the side of the ship
was cut open, and the four poor fellows were liberated from
a floating sepulchre, after an entombment of three days
and three nights in the mighty deep.

" The spot where the vessel struck is called Porthellick,
in the island of St. Mary's, Scilly : she must have been
driven on the rocks soon after midnight, at about the
period of high-water, and was discovered lying dry at
about seven o'clock on Thursday morning, by a man
accidentally passing along the cliffs. In another half-hour
the returning tide would have sealed their fate. The body
of VINCENT was thrown on the rocks at a short distance from
the wreck, and has been interred in the burial-ground of
St. Mary's, with the usual rites of the established church.

" Not the least remarkable part of the narrative is, that
in the afternoon of Wednesday, the 18th, the wreck floating
bottom up was fallen in with, at about a league and a half
distant from the Islands, by two pilot boats, which took her
in tow for about an hour ; but their tow-ropes breaking,
and night approaching, with a heavy sea running and every
appearance of bad weather, they abandoned her ; not
having the least suspicion that there were human beings
alive in the hold of the vessel, which was floating with

little more than her keel above water! whilst, had the vessel not been so taken in tow, the set of the current would have drifted her clear off the islands into the vast Atlantic."¶

The extreme Western horn of Porth Hellick, is Giant's Castle. On the way thither many sepulchral barrows may be noticed on the downs to the North. Borlase's description of the castle itself is so good that it may be transcribed with advantage, though another century has not passed without its effect upon the encampment. The castles on the Cornish cliffs still remain, but we can no more explain the origin of those enclosures, then Dr. Borlase could. "The castle," he wrote, " is situated on a promontory which towards the sea is an immense crag of rocks, as if heaped on each other : this heap or turret of rocks declines also quick, but not so rough towards the land, and then spreads to join the downs, where at the foot of this knoll it has first a ditch crossing the neck of land from sea to sea ; then a low Vallum of the same direction ; next, a second ditch and a higher Vallum ; lastly, near the top of this crag, it had a wall of stone encompassing every part, but where the natural rocks were a sufficient security ; this wall by the ruins appears to have been very high and thick. It is call'd, as I said but now, the Giant's Castle, the common people in these islands as well as elsewhere, attributing all extraordinary works to giants. We have many of these Castles on the Cornish cliffs ; they seem designed by pirates and invaders to protect themselves whilst they were landing their forces, ammunition, and implements of war, and to secure a safe retreat towards their ships in case of need. I am apt therefore to think that such Cliff-Castles are as ancient as the times of the Danish, if not of the Saxon invasions."

¶ This striking narrative was extracted from the first edition of this work by Mr. George H. Lewes, and published in his "Sea-side Studies."

On the Western side of this Carn, just above the cliff, is the Logan Rock, which has the great advantage of being very accessible and easily moved. Its weight is calculated to be forty-five tons.

Not far from the Logan Rock, near half-way down the hill, next the sea, is a cave among the rocks, called Tom Butt's bed, which is very dangerous and difficult to get at, the ground being so steep about it ; it is so called from a boy who concealed himself in it, three days and three nights in the reign of Queen Anne, for fear of being impressed on board a man of war. †

Church Point and Ledge, is the name given to the next mass of rocks projecting into the water. The name is derived from the fact that the outer point of this ledge, when in a line with the old Church, is a mark for pilots.

Blue Carn, the mass of rocks forming the cliff at this part, is usually distinguished as the Inner and the Outer Carn. The Inner is chiefly remarkable for its laminated appearance, the result of horizontal decomposition ; the Outer, more to the South East, is a very singular group of rocks piled upon each other in every variety of form. Almost immediately after Blue Carn, we pass Porth Minick with its white gravelly beach, and arrive at Old Town, whence a road already described leads to Hugh Town.

† Troutbeck.

HISTORY AND SOCIAL CONDITION.

The Scilly Islands have usually been identified with the Cassiterides or Tin Islands, with which the Phœnicians are said to have traded; but as the traces of tin in the islands are very scanty, and there is little evidence that any mines have ever been worked in them, the identification is doubtful. The more certain testimony of names of places, and the numerous barrows, and similar relics found in the islands warrant us in asserting that they were inhabited at an early period by the same Celtic race which occupied Britain. They fell with the mainland under the Roman dominion, and towards the end of the Roman possession, they seem to have been used as a penal settlement for heretics, if not for other offenders. When the limits of the Empire were contracted, Scilly was probably left with very few inhabitants; but there is reason to believe that it was not altogether tenantless. As the country West of the Tamar for a long time remained independent of the Saxons, the Scilly Islands may be supposed to have possessed a similar immunity, and we may believe, that the Christian religion planted there before the Romans withdrew, was preserved during the three or four centuries which elapsed, before we find them again mentioned. Soon after the arrival of the Northmen on the coast of England, these islands re-appear in history. The West Welshmen, or Celts of Cornwall, on more than one occasion, joined the new comers in their attacks on the West Saxons, and the Northmen used the islands as a station whence they issued on their excursions. A very ancient, and credible tradition declares that the islands were subdued by Athelstan, (925-940), and that he founded, *ex voto*, the Collegiate Church of St. Buryan, near the Land's End, on his return from his victorious expedition. The subjugation was necessarily imperfect, and the Saga of King Olaf Tryggvesson tells us, how after a cruise of four. years spent in ravaging the Western coast of England, Scotland, and France, the Viking came (about 980,) to the Scilly Isles, where he met with a christian hermit who had the gift of prophecy, and brought before him many great proofs of the power of the Almighty. In consequence of this Olaf, and his followers, were baptised forthwith. He remained there, continues the Saga, a long time, took the true faith, and got with him priests and other learned men ; and we know that when he returned to Norway a few years after, he laboured to introduce Christianity there, and perished in the troubles which followed. By the time of Edward the Confessor, (1042-1066,) some monks settled in St. Nicholas, (Tresco,) had acquired the tithes of all the islands, and the exclusive ownership of St. Elid's, (St. Helens,) St. Sampson, St. Teon, (Tean,) Reutmen, and Nurcho.† Scilly is not mentioned in Domesday Book ; but we find King Henry making the religious house in Tresco a cell of Tavistock Abbey, to which he annexed all the possessions of the monks. Reginald, the King's natural son, and Earl of Cornwall, confirmed his father's grant, which affords a presumption that the islands were then held as part of the Earldom. The Abbey of Tavistock retained the property thus annexed to it down to the dissolution of Monasteries, and the Abbots were often improperly called the Lords of Scilly. With the exception, however, of the islands already named, and a little land in St. Mary's and Agnes, the group seems to have been always in the hands of laymen. St. Mary's and some others were long in the possession of the Blanchminsters, and afterwards of the Coleshills, as their representatives, by the service of maintaining 12 (10?)

---

† It does not seem possible to identify the last two ; but neither of them was St. Mary's, or St. Agnes.

armed men to keep the Castle, and by the rent of 300
puffins, or 6s. 8d. Agnes was held by the Hamelys, or
Hamleys, apparently as inferior grantees of the Blanchminsters, for a similar length of time. A fortification of
Scilly was included in the large plans formed in the early
part of the reign of Henry VIII., but with many other
similar schemes it was never completed. Upon the dissolution of Monasteries, (1539,) the possessions of the Abbot,
and Monks of Tavistock, were surrendered to the King.
When Leland visited the islands, a few years afterwards, he
found them in very bad condition ; houses had been deserted
and left to go to ruin ; those which were still inhabited
were much dilapidated ; and although the pasture of the
islands was " exceeding good " and the land fertile, " few
men were glad to inhabit them for all their plenty, for
robbers by the sea that took their cattle of force." These
robbers he said were Frenchmen and Spaniards. At that
time Danvers, a gentleman of Wiltshire, and Whittington, a
gentleman of Gloucestershire, were owners of Scilly ; but
they scarcely got 40 marks, (£26 : 13 : 4,) a year out of
the islands. Danvers and Whittington were the representatives of the Coleshills ; it does not appear how the estate
of the Hamley family had been extinguished.

It was one of the articles of accusation against Thomas,
Lord Seymour, the Admiral, and brother of the Lord
Protector, that he had gotten into his hands the strong and
dangerous isles of Scilly, to further his ambitious designs,
and on his attainder, the islands fell into the hands of the
Crown, *jure ducatus*. The statement made by Dr. Borlase,
on the authority of a MS. of Anstis, the Garter King, that
the Crown became possessed of Scilly, in the reign of Mary
by exchange, may be dismissed as erroneous. In 1549, the
name of Godolphin first occurs in connection with Scilly,
as that of the Captain of the group, and in 1571, Elizabeth
leased the islands to (Sir) Francis Godolphin for 38 years,
upon condition that he defended them and paid a yearly
rental of £10 to the Receiver of the Duchy. This lease was
opposed by Mr. Edward Bukeley, who asserted that the

Lord Admiral Seymour had purchased only the moiety of the islands held by Danvers, and had wrongfully ousted the representatives of Whittington from the other half. He alleged that he was entitled by descent to the share of one of the six co-heirs of Whittington, and that he had compounded with, or purchased the shares of, the other co-partners, out whatever else he may have gained by his claim, it is certain that the possession of Sir Francis Godolphin was not disturbed.

In 1604, before the expiration of the first term, James I. granted a lease in reversion to Sir William Godolphin, for fifty years, at a rental of £20 ; and in 1636, Charles I., granted another reversionary lease to Francis Godolphin, for 50 years, at a rental of £40. This last lease would have expired in 1709 ; but in 1698, William III. granted Sidney, Lord Godolphin, a third lease in reversion for eighty-nine years, at the same rental, and on the expiration of this, the Duke of Leeds, the representative of the Godolphin family, obtained another lease of thirty-one years from the year 1800, at the same rent of £40. It is not easy to see what validity any of these leases, except the last, possessed, as not one of them was within the leasing powers granted by Parliament to the successive Dukes of Cornwall ; but however that may be, the Godolphin, and Godolphin-Osborne, families retained possession of the islands for two hundred and sixty years, the interregnum excepted. In 1593, the Star Castle was built under the direction, it would seem, of Sir Francis Godolphin, but at the expense of the Crown ; and in 1628, during the war with France, Dutch engineers were employed in fortifying the islands. In 1637, Dr. Bastwick, for his vigorous denunciations of Episcopacy, was transported, by order of the Star Chamber, after having been subjected to infamous and degrading punishments, to Scilly, there to remain imprisoned until he made submission ; but in 1640, he was conveyed to London and released by order of the Parliament. In the civil war which followed, the islands were held for the King, long after the rest of England was brought under the authority of Parliament.

In March, 1646, when all Cornwall, except Pendennis Castle, had been subdued by Fairfax, the Prince of Wales fled from Pendennis to Scilly, but after a short stay of six weeks he escaped to Guernsey. Lady Fanshawe, who accompanied her husband in the Prince's suite, has left us a graphic picture of the misery and discomfort she suffered from bad lodging and scanty food, from the time when she landed, wet, very sick, and big with child, to the time when the party left for the Channel Islands. Sir John Granville remained in charge of Scilly as Governor on behalf of the King, and long continued to harrass the merchant shipping when cause led them near him. At length, in 1651, an expedition was fitted out under the command of Admiral Blake and Sir George Ayscue, to reduce the islands to subjection. Tresco was first seized on the night of the 18th of April,† and soon after a landing was effected on St Mary's ; the garrison in Star Castle were speedily brought to great straits, and Sir John Granville, with eight hundred men, surrendered themselves prisoners.

Upon the Restoration, the possession of Scilly was resumed by the Godolphin family, and thenceforwards there is little note-worthy in the annals of the islands. We find them used once more as a place of transportation in 1681, when seven unfortunate Popish Priests were conveyed thither from Newgate ; but the default of stirring events is amply compensated by the full details of the social history of Scilly, which have been preserved. The political enquirer may find in the successive fortunes of the group, an interesting study in miniature. The Godolphin family steadily rose in power and importance, and it was not probable that a Lord-Treasurer, or other great officer of State, could attend to the management of the distant and worthless property, of which he was lessee. The limited nature of his own interest disabled him, moreover, from

† A day was lost through the treachery of a pilot named Nance, who, though " the most knowing pilot " of the place, conducted the landing party to Northwethel, " affirming on his life" it was Tresco ; surprised, and exposed to the enemy's fire, the party retreated to Tean.

granting long under-leases, even when the term he possessed was not the subject of settlement. Scilly was thus held by an absentee, with a partial estate. The leases, moreover, conferred on the lessees conclusive jurisdiction in all plaints and causes ; heresies, treasons, matters of life and limb, and Admiralty questions, excepted. The lessee, or as he was then, and is still, termed the Lord Proprietor, accordingly created a court of twelve, who were little scrupulous about the limits of their power. At one time, we find them issuing an order prohibiting masters of vessels from importing strangers, or exporting residents, under a penalty of ten pounds ; at another time, a troublesome thief is ordered to be put on board the first of his Majesty's ships of war which might call ; women were ducked at the Quay-head ; and men and women were ordered to be publicly whipped. Till near the end of the last century, the spiritual care of the islands was entrusted to a solitary Chaplain, appointed by the Proprietor, and receiving a small stipend from him, who resided on St. Mary's; " on the other islands " says Heath " four teachers, who are fisher- men, are appointed to read prayers, and preach in their respective Churches according to the doctrine of the Church of England. They are men chosen for their exemplary morals, and are no ill grace to the pulpit. Their reward is their reputation, and they practice goodness for esteem." It is possible that the islands increased in prosperity immediately after the Restoration, and we know that St. Martin's, which had been deserted, was re-populated. Heath, however, quotes a manuscript, written about 1717, which refers to the improper conduct of the local steward, and speaks of the effect of the precarious tenure of the actual cultivators as discouraging any improvement of land. Heath himself lived at Scilly throughout the year 1744 ; he alludes to the enormous power wielded by the agent, but describes him as a person " esteemed for his generosity, good sense, and humanity." Elsewhere, he says " there being no owners of houses, or lands in Scilly, the people's hindrances in the improvement of land and trade, are the short leases, and scarcity of houses to be met with," and we find him quoting a proverb " a feast or a famine in Scilly," as an illustration of the temper of the inhabitants. When Troutbeck was Chaplain of the Islands fifty years later, Scilly had evidently retrograded. In his survey are many notices of the arbitrary conduct of successive Stewards,* and as the then Duke of Leeds was engrossed in political life (he was for sometime Secretary of State,) it was almost impossible to obtain access to him. The Church was going to ruin for want of necessary repairs, and the parsonage which Troutbeck had patched up at his own expense, without being able to get any allowance made for his outlay, was threatened with destruction by the encroachment of the sea. Rents were unaltered, and it began to be regarded as a matter of right that they should not be changed ; a few acres farmed by a father were split up on his death amongst his sons ; the population rapidly increased, the standard of living fell, and the islands degenerated into a little Ireland. When Woodley wrote, in 1822, things were even worse, the doom of pauperism seemed to have fastened on Scilly. There had been Government grants, charitable subscriptions, bounties for fishing, salt allowed to be used free of duty, encouragement toward making kelp, all to little purpose, for every Winter there was the deepest distress, sometimes amounting to famine. Upon the expiration of the current lease, in 1831, the Duke of Leeds declined to renew it upon the terms proposed by the Duchy, and the islands remained for a year or two in the hands of William IV. Some steps were taken to ameliorate their condition during this interval ; the building of a new Church, and of a new and enlarged pier were commenced ; but luckily for the islands they were soon leased again to a lessee, whose energy has totally changed their condition.

---

* One instance may be quoted. Kelp-making had been introduced in the islands, and the Steward asserted, and for some years exercised, a right of pre-emption of the kelp made at less than half its market price.

The lessee in question, Mr. A. SMITH, the late M.P. for
Truro, took the islands for a term of three lives, paying a
fine and accepting the obligation of completing the works
which had been begun. The honourable member is a
Liberal, but in Scilly he is a wise and benevolent autocrat.
Circumstances favoured his enterprise. Taking the islands
just after the Reform Bill, he has had all the benefit of the
free-trade legislation which has so enormously increased
our foreign trade, and made Scilly a place of continuous
ship-building. The silent revolution of steam, again, has
brought the islands close to the home markets, and converted large portions of them into gardens, whence London
is supplied with the earliest potatoes. Lastly, though many
a lord of a manor exercises ownership over large parishes,
there is generally some little freeholder who is the fly in
his ointment, and at the last his border is reached, whence
a recalcitrant tenant may grin at him over the hedge ; the
lessee of Scilly has the satisfaction of knowing that thirty
miles of sea separate him from his nearest neighbour. But
circumstances would have availed little without a resident
landlord possessing a cool head and firm hand. Mr. Smith,
at the outset, built himself a house close to the ruins of the
Abbey, where he has resided the greater part of each year
since he has been in possession. Next, the fields were con-
solidated into moderate holdings ; those who were dis-
possessed were ordered to turn to other occupations, or to
seek a wider field for their energies in the neighbouring
county. Paupers were resolutely deported to the mainland.
The population being thus reduced, any attempt to increase
it was strictly watched. It is not known that any order
prescribed the number of children permissible in a family,
but their destination in life was carefully controlled. If a
farmer showed a tendency to keep two or three sons about
him, he was warned that one was sufficient for the farm,—
let the others be one a shipwright, one a sailor, and a fourth
might go to Penzance, and be an artisan or a tradesman ; if
the farmer objected, the passage to Cornwall was open to·

all, and his year expired next Michaelmas. Schools have been established. Roads have been made by a species of *corvee*. The council of twelve still exists, but their power is slight where the lessee resides. The effect of this paternal superintendence has been the transformation of pauperism into prosperity. The population has been considerably reduced, and there may be said to be now no poor amongst them. Land has been brought into cultivation which formerly lay barren; ship-building has been increased, and a fleet of vessels hailing from Scilly help to maintain the carrying trade of the empire.

One effect of the increased prosperity of the islands has been a considerable rise in the prices of provisions, as will be seen from the following table :—

	1744. Heath.	1796. Troutbeck.	1822. Woodley.	1850. North.	1865.
Beef per lb...	2½d.	3d. to 4d.	4d.	5½d.	
Mutton ——	2½d.to3d.	3d. to 1d.	4d. to 4½d.	6d. (scarce.)	
Lamb ——	10d. a qr.	3d. to 4d.	4d.	7d.	
Veal ——	Variable.	3d.	....	....	
Pork ——	2½d. to 3d.	3d.	3½d.	....	
Butter from Cornwall ...	Scarce.	Scarce.	1s. 3d. to 1s. 4d.	10d. to 1s.	
Potatoes per bushel of 24 gallons......	....	....	2s. 6d. to 3s.	....	
Apples per 100	....	....	2s. 6d. to 4s.	....	
A Goose (about 5½ lbs.)	...... 1s. in Summer 2s. 6d. to 3s. at Xmas.		2s. 6d.	....	
Rabbits per couple......	1s.	1s.	....	....	
Live ducks do.	......	......	1s. 4d. to 1s. 6d.	....	
Live fowls do.	1s.	1s.	1s. 2d. to 1s. 4d.	....	
Eggs per doz.	2½d.	3d.	3d. to 4d.	4d. to 6d.	
A turbot	1s. 6d.	......	1s. 6d. to 2s. 6d.	....	
Soles per pair	......	......	1s. 6d.		
Cod-fish	....	......	9d. to 1s.	....	
do. cured per lb............	1½d. to 2d.	......	3d.	2½d.	
Ling do.	4d. to 6d.	......	4½d.	....	
Mullet	....	......	....	6d.	
Lobsters (each.) ..		......	6d. to 8d.	....	
Crabs (small)	......	......	1d.	....	

It must, however, be mentioned that the supply of fresh fish is uncertain, and the beef and mutton produced on the islands is small, and the beef of inferior quality. The regular communication between Scilly and Penzance, ensured by the " Little Western" steamer, has caused a considerable importation of butchers' meat from the latter place, and as great an exportation of eggs, poultry, and fish thither. The absence of all statistics of wages must be attributed to the fact that hired labourers have never existed as a class in Scilly. We may conclude this chapter with a short notice of the taxation borne by the inhabitants, which is somewhat anomalous. It may be said that at one time no Imperial taxes were levied in the islands; whether this happened because it was thought that the amount which might be collected would not defray the cost of collection, or from some notion that Scilly enjoyed an immunity like the Channel Islands, and the Isle of Man, cannot be determined. In 1696, a Custom House was erected in consequence of the representations of Capt. John Crudge, whose connection with the Godolphin family has been elsewhere stated, apparently to prevent frauds on the Revenue on the mainland, but no question as to the legality of its erection seems to have been raised. From that time the Customs have been received by the officers appointed for that purpose. No Excise Duties have ever been levied; in Heath's time everyone malted as he pleased, and though the practice has been discontinued, it was left off, as we believe, in consequence of the inferior quality of the beer thus home-made. No Licence Duties are paid, no Property or Assessed Taxes are collected, and the islands were never assessed to the Land Tax. Before the new Poor Law, collections at the Church, and some small charges on shipping were applied to the relief of the poor; Scilly is now a part of the Penzance Union, and a small poor-rate is levied. This poor-rate, an occasional road-rate, and landing dues at the pier are the only imposts to which the islanders are subject. We do not pretend to explain by what authority some taxes are levied, and others omitted ; were the matter of sufficient importance it might be made the subject of considerable argument in courts of law ; it is sufficient here to state the facts for the information of the reader.

BIRDS.

LAND BIRDS.

Mr. E. H. Rodd, of Penzance, has furnished us with his notes of rare and remarkable birds, observed at Scilly up to the present time, incorporated in this appendix.

Of the Birds of Prey. Some of the British Hawks are permanently resident, such as the Sparrow Hawk and Kestrel; the Peregrine Falcon is also a resident at Scilly, and breeds on some of the precipitous cliffs. The Osprey, Marsh Harrier, Common Harrier, and Montagu's Harrier have also occurred in the islands.

In 1849, a rare Owl was obtained from Scilly, in the Scops-eared Owl, (*Strix Scops.*) This bird is remarkable for its diminutive size, and also for the beautifully pencilled brown and grey shadings of its plumage. The Short-eared Owl, (*Strix Brachyotos*), periodically visits the islands, appearing with Woodcocks in the Autumn, and during the past Winter, a large number of the Long-eared Owl occurred at Tresco.

A mature specimen of the rarest of the three British Shrikes, (*Laniadæ*), the Woodchat, (*Lanius Rufus*), was caught in a fishing boat near the islands, in the spring of 1840.* In 1849, several specimens of the young of the year were obtained. The adult specimen, and also one in immature plumage, are preserved in the collection of Mr. Rodd.

* See preface to Yarrell's British Birds.

The rose-coloured Starling, (*Pastor Roseus*), another rare species, has been obtained from the islands ; * and in the year 1847, several instances of the Hoopoe, (*Upupa Epops*), were captured.†

The Turtle Dove, (*Columba Turtur*), is commonly observed in the Summer months ; and the Stock Dove, (*Columba Œnas*), has, in two instances, been obtained from the islands. The Ring Dove, Rock Dove, and Turtle Dove are recorded in the Cornish Fauna, whilst the Stock Dove has been only known of late years.

The Golden Oriole, another rare bird, was captured at Tresco, in the Spring of this year, and two others seen ; it was also observed in the years 1848 and 1849; its remarkable and brilliant yellow plumage, with black wings, renders its occurrence easily observed anywhere.

In the Autumnal migration are occasionally observed the three British species of Willow Wrens, (*Sylviadæ*), viz. : the Wood Wren, the common Willow Wren, and the Chiff-chaff. The former species is unknown in the West of Cornwall; the whole family are lovely in form, and delicate in their habits and pursuits. Most of the British migratory Warblers have been observed at Scilly in their migratorial movements, but not the Nightingale. Amongst these may be mentioned the Reed Wren, Lesser White-throat, Red-starts, Garden Warblers, Black-caps, Pied Fly-catchers, and very frequently the Gold Crested Wrens are seen in large numbers. Amongst the rare British Land Birds obtained at Scilly, two deserve special notice, viz : the Red-breasted Fly-catcher, killed in October, 1863, and another in the Autumn of 1865, and the Short-toe'd Lark, killed in September, 1853. A specimen of Pallas's Sand Grouse was picked up dead at St. Agnes, in 1863, a species unknown to England before that period.

Amongst the company of migratorial visitants, the Wryneck, (*Yunx Torquilla*), unknown as a Spring visitant in Cornwall, was captured at the same time. Quails are occasionally seen on the isles, and Landrails may be found every Summer.

* See Yarrell's British Birds, vol. ii, p. 52.

† Ibid., vol. ii, p. 171.

In this brief reference to the rarer Land-birds, it has not been thought necessary to attempt a minute history of the ornithology of the isles ; the usual way-side birds will be recognised by every observer.

We may close this section with a curious extract from the Journal of Gilbert White, of Selbourne, published by Yarrell in his article upon the Woodcock, " a gentleman writes word from St. Mary's, Scilly, that in the night between the 10th and 11th of the month, the wind being West, there fell such a flight of Woodcocks within the walls of the garrison, that he himself shot, and conveyed home, twenty-six couple, besides three couple which he wounded, but did not give himself the trouble to retrieve. On the following day, the 12th, the wind continuing West, he found but few. This person further observes, that Easterly and Northerly winds only have usually been remarked as propitious in bringing Woodcocks to the Scilly Islands. So that he is totally at a loss to account for this Western flight, unless they came from Ireland. As they took their departure in the night between the 11th and 12th, the wind still continuing West, he supposes they were gone to make a visit to the counties of Cornwall and Devonshire. From circumstances in the letter, it appears that the ground within the lines of the garrison abounds with furze. Some Woodcocks settled in the street of St. Mary's, and ran into the houses and out-houses."* The isles are annually visited towards the Autumn by considerable numbers of this choice and favourite bird.

WATER BIRDS.

The breeding season, in May and June, is the best time for watching sea-birds. The attention of the naturalist will be caught by cries from the wild hoarse-scream and " kuckle " of the various gulls, the mingled sounds of the Puffins, Razor-bills, Guillemots, Oyster-catchers, Shags, Terns, &c., to the tiny musical whistle of the Ring Plover.

* See Yarrell's British Birds, vol. ii, pp. 586-7.

Perhaps the most interesting and the most beautiful family of Birds which frequent our isles, is that of the Terns, (*Sturnidæ*), nearly all of which breed annually on the grass banks, sands, and shingle, at the different isles, and especially at Annet. The Terns are remarkable for their light and elegant forms, and for the unsullied purity of their white and light blue plumage.

The Roseate Tern, (*Sterna Dougallii*), especially deserves the attention of the visitor, as presenting, more particularly in the breeding season, a most delicate and lovely rose-coloured tint on the breast, varying in intensity in certain lights, and exhibiting a peculiarly beautiful, glowing, hectic blush. This colour is so delicate and evanescent that it quickly disappears after death, if the skin is exposed to a strong light. Besides the Roseate, the Common, Sandwich and Arctic Tern, are met with. And in May, 1852, an adult specimen of a rare species, the Gull-billed Tern, was obtained from Scilly, the first Cornish specimen. Their eggs are all similar in general appearance, the colour being clay-yellow, blotched, and spotted with black.

The most remarkable Gull is the Great Black-backed Gull, (*Larus marinus*), the largest of our species which annually breeds on the high rocks of Gorregan. The Lesser Black-backed Gull and the Herring Gull also breed at Scilly ; the eggs of the two latter are so similar in size and colouring that it is almost impossible to distinguish them. The Great Black-backed Gull is restless and angry in the breeding season ; and hovering beyond gun-shot above her nest seeks to scare away intruders by her wild, hoarse scream.

Amongst the Heron tribe the Spoon-bill, (*Platalea Leucorodia*), is an occasional visitor. A specimen of this bird has been killed at Tresco. It was without the plumes which adorn the adult bird. In the last week of May, 1850, another specimen was shot at St. Mary's. Of this Mr. Rodd writes, " It is by far the most adult of all the examples that have come under my notice as Cornish specimens. The occipital crest is developed, which has not been the case in others that I have seen, and there are other marks which denote its being an old and mature bird."

One of the most beautiful of the British Herons has been captured on the Isles, viz., the Squacco Heron, (*Ardea Comata*). This bird was observed in a great many instances in the Land's End district during 1849.

A specimen of the Night Heron, (*Ardea Nycticorax*), in beautiful plumage, with three long, subulated, snow-white feathers, proceeding from the back of the head, was obtained in 1849.

The large Curlew, Turnstones, Oyster-catchers, the latter generally known by the name of Sea-pies, are constant residents; while the Common Sandpiper and the Red-shank Sandpiper have both been seen. The Oyster-catchers and Ring Dotterels breed at Scilly; and their eggs may be found, without difficulty, on the loose shingle above high-water mark, with scarcely any preparation of a nest, except a slight indentation. The Ring Dotterel's egg is very beautiful, both in shape and in the arrangement of its colours. From its general resemblance to the sea-shore pebbles, which is also characteristic of the Terns' and Oyster Catchers' eggs, a casual observer would probably never notice them. Eggs of the Ring Dotterel have been obtained in April, showing how early this bird breeds. One of our rarer British Birds, the little Ringed Plover, was obtained from Tresco, in 1863, and another equally valuable, the Brown Snipe or Longbeak, the first and only Cornish specimen, was obtained from St. Mary's, in October, 1857. It has not been clearly ascertained that the Turnstone has bred at Scilly, although its appearance in Summer makes it probable.

Guillemots, Razor-bills, Puffins, Storm Petrels, Common Shearwaters, all breed on the isles. The Common

Guillemot, (*Uria Troile*), is remarkable for two properties in its egg : the first is, that although the bird itself is not larger than a Bantam fowl, the egg is as large as that of a Turkey ; the second property is that no two eggs are alike. They vary from a light verdigris green to white, more or less, and sometimes not at all, spotted with black.

The Canada Goose has been shot in the isles ;[*] the Puffin, or Sea-Parrot, is more common than on the coast of Cornwall.[†] " *Puffinus major* is very well known to the Scillonians, by whom it is called *Hackbolt*. They inform me it is a constant visitant in the latter part of Autumn, and represent its manners on the water as resembling those of *P. anglorum*, [‡] the Manx Shearwater."

In the same valuable work there is an interesting account of the Manx, or Common Shearwater, written by the late Mr. D. W. Mitchell, who visited Scilly in pursuit of ornithological science ; and afterwards held an important position in the Zoological Society of London.

"To the Westward of St. Agnes, in the Scilly group, lies a barren island called Annet. Its Northern shore is abrupt and craggy ; it gradually slopes towards the South, and narrows into a sort of peninsula, where the sandy soil is rich enough to produce a dense growth of short ferns. Here is the strong-hold of the Shearwaters. Sit down on a rock which commands the little territory, and you will see nothing but the Terns, who have a station on the higher and central part of the island. You may wait all a sunny day in June, but not a Shearwater will you see on land or water. There are plenty near you all the time, however, as you may ascertain by the odour which issues from the first burrow you look into among the ferns. As soon as the sun is down you will see a little party of five or six flitting silently across the sound, or steering out to sea. The latest fishers from the colony of Terns are coming home from the sandy

---

* Yarrell, vol. iii. p. 92.　　† Ibid., vol. iii. p. 363.

‡ Ibid., vol., iii. pp. 504-5.

shallows, five or six miles away, with their throats and beaks crammed with Lance-fish, when the Shearwaters begin to wake. You will not see them come out of their holes ; you first catch sight of them skimming round the corner of a rock close to the water. Perhaps they will have a great gathering, such as I encountered one evening in Smith's Sound. There was a congregation of at least three hundred, in the middle of the tide-way, washing, dipping, preening feathers, and stretching wings, evidently just awake, and making ready for the night's diversion. As I wanted a few specimens more than I had dug out of the burrows, I ran my boat well up to them, and when they rose, got as many as I wished, besides a few unfortunate cripples who were only winged, and proved, by their agility in swimming and diving, a good deal too much for my boatmen. I think a good dog would have no chance with them. They allowed me to come quite close. They sit low in the water ; they make no noise when disturbed, though in their holes they are eloquent enough, the Scillonian synonyms of *Crew* and *Cockathodon* being derived from the guttural melodies they pour forth as the spade approaches the end in which the egg is deposited."* The reader will find other interesting details respecting this bird in Yarrell.

The Storm Petrel,† the smallest web-footed bird which braves our stormy seas out of sight and apparent reach of land, lays its two beautiful white eggs, encircled with a zone of rufous yellow towards the larger end, under cover of the over-hanging rocks of the more inaccessible islets. Mr. Rodd thus describes the habits of this little mariner, as he observed them during a fishing excursion in Mount's Bay.

" In the summer of 1834, when at a distance of six or seven miles from shore, in Mount's Bay, fishing, on a per-fectly calm summer's evening, ten or twelve Stormy Petrels, just before sunset, continued flying about our boat,

---

* Yarrell, p.p. 509, 510. † Ibid., vol. iii. p. 525.

apparently regardless of men or of any danger. We several times endeavoured to strike them with our oars ; but, instead of exhibiting caution, the bird just struck at would fly almost in our faces and around our heads : and if we could have kept the boat stationary, I am certain they might have been caught by the hand. They continued hawking about with an abrupt and wavering flight, not unlike that of the Bank Swallow, sometimes near the surface of the sea, at other times pausing on the surface, touching, but not alighting on the water ; then mounting up to the height of eight or ten feet, and wheeling to and fro, evidently watching the surface of the water, and perhaps the little insects and flies which sport about at this season of the year at a distance from land. They appeared at times to be in pursuit of moving objects, as they were dodging and turning continually and abruptly, like the swallow-tribe. Now and then they appeared to take a momentary rest upon the water ; but they were instantly up again, fanning the surface and sporting about as before. I never observed, in any instance, their wings entirely closed when on the water ; nor did I perceive any positive swimming action. Their alighting resembled the action of gulls, when they dip in the sea suddenly and rise again, pausing only to secure an object of food."

The most common of the Sanderlings, generally so called, is the Dunlin, (*Tringa variabilis*), a bird remarkable for the change which its plumage undergoes in the Summer and Winter months. During the Summer the back of the bird is dark, with rufous edges, and the belly has across it an irregular patch of black. In the Winter the whole of the upper plumage is ash-grey, and all the under parts are pure white.

Mr. Mitchell succeeded in capturing, when at the Isles, one of the rarest British birds, called the Pectoral Sandpiper, (*Tringa pectoralis*), a species scarcely known in the British Isles ; and this specimen is now in the British Museum. This bird was submitted to Mr. Yarrell's inspection ; and he has referred minutely to this example, in his

work on British Birds, under the article, Pectoral Sandpiper. " D. W. Mitchell, Esq., of Penzance, sent me in
June, 1840, a coloured drawing of the natural size, and a
fully detailed description, with measurements of a Sandpiper, shot by himself on the 27th of the previous month,
while the bird was resting on some sea-weed within a few
yards of the water, on the rocky shore of Annet, one of the
uninhabited islands at Scilly. On the following day
another example was seen, but became so wild after an
unsuccesful shot, that it took off to another island and
escaped altogether. The close accordance of the specimen
obtained, with the description of *Tringa pectoralis* in
Summer plumage in the Fourth Part of M. Temminck's
Manual, led Mr. Mitchell to a true conclusion as to the
species and its novelty and interest in this country."*

The following interesting note on the Manx Shearwater
is due to J. N. R. Millett, Esq., of Penzance :—" During a
visit to the isles, in 1826, I tried for several successive
days, to get a shot at the Shearwaters, but in vain. They
invariably kept just out of gun-shot, and I began to despair
of success. I heard, however, accidentally, that flocks of
these birds were daily seen about noon, sitting quietly on
the water in St. Mary's Sound. Thither I proceeded without delay, and found numerous groups of them scattered
about in the tide-way, evidently reposing after their morning's
fishing at sea. They allowed me to approach within gun-shot
without any apparent alarm, when I succeeded in obtaining
some choice specimens. In crossing the Sound on several
occasions afterwards, about the same hour of the day, I
invariably witnessed similar gatherings of these birds : and
from the fact of never having, before or since, seen a single
bird of this description *on the water*, although I have seen
very many on the wing, and at various distances from land,
I am led to infer that the habit of the Shearwater is to
remain at rest, and probably asleep, on the water during
the mid-day, the period of digestion, and to confine their
fishing exclusively to to the morning and evening. "

* Yarrell, vol. 2, p. 655.

FERNS.*

The grand botanical feature of Scilly, is that most beautiful and very interesting species, *Asplenium marinum*, or Sea Spleenwort. It attains, among its spray-washed rocks, a luxuriance nowhere else to be met with in Britain ; and, probably, not excelled in any part of Europe.

In the fissures of rocks, which form those peculiar carns or promontories which radiate in every direction, and are so remarkable a feature of the islands, this fern grows most superbly, attaining to the length of nearly thirty-three inches. At Peninis, Porth Hellick, and other parts of the South Coast of St. Mary's, it is the most abundant : but it is everywhere met with ; the usual length of the fronds being twelve, fifteen, or twenty inches. The fronds are generally fertile, and often in confluent fruit. Its roots are black and brittle ; and penetrate far into the crevices of the rocks, (which are chiefly of the very coarsest granite, and which, therefore, readily decompose,) and are attached so firmly that the plants are not obtained without much patience and difficulty.

The difficulty, if not the impossibility, of cultivating this species in the open air, away from the sea, is too well known to need comment : † but it luxuriates in the stove,

* Principally compiled from the notes of E. W. Cooke, Esq., R.A., F.R.S.

† The genera of Trichomanes and Hymenophyllum, also requiring perpetual moisture, can only be cultivated under bell-glasses or in ward-cases ; and these are, perhaps, of still more difficult culture.

and will bear any degree of heat, if accompanied by moist
atmosphere. Specimens obtained in Scilly, and planted in
a hot-house between masses of sand-stone, have grown
beautifully and borne fruit abundantly.

Asplenium lanceolatum, a species whose habitat must be
sought also, with few exceptions, near the sea-coast, grows
in St. Agnes. Some specimens, found near the Light-
house, were so much smaller than the Cornish species, and
presented so distinct a character, that they may perhaps be
considered as constituting a variety. Most of the fronds
were fertile.

Asplenium adiantum nigrum, or Black Spleenwort, is
also found in St. Agnes.

W. Cooke states his impression that he found *Asplenium
ruta-muraria* growing on a stone wall between Hugh-town
and Holy Vale.

Lastræa recurva, so abundant in the West of
Cornwall, was only met in one spot in St. Mary's.

Osmunda regalis, our royal flowering fern, is very
abundant in one (and perhaps the only) locality, viz., the
Marsh near Old Town, St. Mary's. In this spot, intersected
as it is with water, this noble fern spreads over a considerable tract of swampy ground, attaining a very large size.
The rich, amber colour of its luxuriant foilage presents, in
the Autumn, a most charming effect. Numerous small
plants, dispersed amidst the larger ones, and equally
fertile, present all the characters which belong to the
Osmunda gracile of North America, being most exquisitely
and delicately formed.

In the Marsh also occur *Lastræa filix-mas*, *Lastræa
dilitata*, and *Lastræa spinulosa*, together with *Asplenium
filix fœmina*, in great profusion. The two former species
are generally distributed in St. Mary's.

Polypodium vulgare is abundant on walls. It is very
large and fine at Holy Vale.

Scolopendrium officinarum, or common Hart's-tongue, exceedingly common in West Cornwall, is only found in one or two wells in the islands.

Pteris Aquilina is generally distributed, but small.

The following is a list of the different genera and species which Mr. Cooke found here :—

Osmunda Regalis, *Royal or Flowering Fern.*
Asplenium marinum, *Sea Spleen-wort.*
————— adiantum nigrum, *Black-hair'd maiden.*
————— ruta muraria, *Wall-rue fern.*
————— lanceolatum, *Hudson's Spleen-wort.*
————— filix-fœmina, *Lady-fern.*
Lastrœa filix-mas, *Male-fern.*
————— recurva, *Bree's-fern.*
————— dilatata, *Broad-shield fern.*
————— spinulosa, *a variety of the preceding.*
Polystichum lobatum, *Prickly fern.*
————— angulare, *a variety of the preceding.*
Polypodium vulgare, *Common poly-pody.*
Scolopendrium officinarum, *Common hart's-tongue.*
Pteris aquilina, *Common brake.*

A GENERAL VIEW OF THE
ZOOLOGICAL FEATURES
OF THE SEA ROUND THE SCILLY ISLANDS.[*]

The granitic formation of these islands is very unfavourable to the zoologist. Comparatively few animals live on these sterile parts of our earth's crust. The reasons of this are easily to be found in the chemical composition of the granite, of which Silica amounts to seventy-five per cent. (in Cornish granite according to Sir Henry De la Beche); in the great resistance which it offers to the dissolving power of wind and weather; both qualities, unfavourable to the maintenance of animal life. The very subordinate presence of lime (chalk, &c.,) of which a great amount is wanted in building shells or crusts, may be stated as one of the most obvious reasons why only few animals live in granitic districts.

The second condition, perhaps the first in importance, on which the peculiarity of a Fauna depends, is the climate. The Isles of Scilly are situated a little to the West of the sixth degree of Western longitude, and exactly in the fiftieth degree of Northern latitude. These islands are therefore, the Channel Islands excepted, the most Southern parts of the United Kingdom. The mean temperature in Summer is 58 degrees, and in Winter

[*] Condensed from a paper contributed by N. Victor Carus, Esq., M.D., to the first edition of this work. The reader may refer to Sea-side Studies (Scilly), by Mr. G. H. Lewes, Blackwood, 1858.

45 degrees. The prevalent wind is South-west or West-
south-west. The climatical conditions are, therefore, very
favourable ; and, whenever the Rennel current permits it,
we may expect to find even Southern forms swept in by the
Atlantic waves. These same stragglers are found on the
Cornish coast, the Fauna of which has been so admirably
worked out.

The last, and not the least important fact, connected
with the distribution of Zoological forms round a coast is
the strength of the tide. Reports of well experienced
pilots and other intelligent seafaring men state that neap
tides run one and a half to two miles an hour; spring tides
three. This is the rate in the adjacent ocean, the tide
gaining much greater, even much more than double this
strength in the numerous channels which separate the
islands one from another. The height of neap tides is
twelve, of spring tides eighteen feet, although the latter of
course have a variation of several feet, so that the littoral
zone has a range from twenty to twenty-four feet.

It is perhaps worth mentioning, for the use of naturalists,
that the statements on the nature of the ground in *Græme
Spence's* map are always very correct, and they may pay
particular attention to their dredge when they find in the
chart an " r " in the midst of " ssh," " s," " gr," etc.
At other places, however, this " r " does not signify rocks,
which might endanger the dredging, but merely stony
ground, as for instance in the North Channel or Broad
Sound, where one may fill the dredge with stones without
losing it. The best ground is the North-eastern, Eastern,
and Southern side of the islands ; but a greater variety of
species has been found by examining the shore at low water
than by dredging. Next, or perhaps equally productive,
was the laminarian zone, the second in depth ; and it is
perhaps worth remarking that some animals have been
found at low-water mark, or even higher, which commonly
inhabit deeper water.

In this paper, mention will be made of the rarer or more
characteristic forms only.

Among the *Fishes*, the Lancelet, (*Amphioxus lanceolatus*) is the most interesting species. Dr. Carus found two specimens at the Northern side of the Seven Stones, in forty fathoms, two others off the Southern coast of St. Agnes, in twenty-five fathoms, and a fifth off the Creeb, in the Road, in three fathoms. Of the other fishes, some belong to the West European seas in common, as the grey Gurnard, (*Trigla Gurnardus*) ; the Mackerel, (*Scomber scomber*) ; the Shan, (*Blennius pholis*) ; the Hake, (*Morlucius vulgaris*) ; the Sole, (*Solea vulgaris*) ; the Plaice ; different species of *Pleuronectes* ; the Conger, (*Conger vulgaris*) ; and others, which are all more or less common at Scilly ; others are representative rather of the South British Fauna, as the common Sea Bream, (*Pagellus centrodontus*) ; the Sandsmelt, (*Atherina presbyter*) ; the Pilchard, (*Clupea pilchardus*) ; and so on ; lastly some, which occur all round the coast, though rarer than those first mentioned, as the Sun-fish, (*Orthagoriscus mola*) ; the Cornish and spotted Sucker, (*Lepadogaster Cornubiencis*), and (*bimaculatus*), and some others, which are comparatively rare in the South, though abundant in the North, as the Cod, (*Gadus Morrhua*) ; the Lumpsucker, (*Cyclopterus lumpus*) ; the Herring, (*Clupea Harengus*). Of great economical importance, are the Scad, (*Caranx trachurus*) ; the Conger, the Ling, (*Lota molva*) ; which are taken in great numbers, and dried and preserved as Winter stores.

The greater number of *Shellfishes* were found between tide marks. Beyond these, there were only the *Patella pellucida* in the laminarian roots, some minute species of *Anomia* in deeper water, and some few of the almost microscopical univalves. The Limpet, (*Patella vulgata*), occurs on many places even beyond high-water mark. It does not appear that there exists a specific difference between those higher growing limpets, and those nearer low-water mark, but the fishermen despise the higher ones as coarse bait, which no reasonable fish would take. It abounds all round the isles, and is frequently used as bait, and even as food ; but even scalloped limpets would not suite a refined palate. Equally abundant on rocks is *Turbo littoreus*, the Periwinkle, and *Trochus ziziphinus*, and *umbilicatus*, whilst Cockles, Scallops, Razor-shells, and Queens, are found in the sandy flats of Tresco and St. Martin's, though scarcer than the former.

There is also a pretty large number of naked Molluscs, found either between tide-marks, on rocks, or in deeper water. They mostly belong to the genera *Doris*, *Eolis*, *Hermœa*, *Triopa*, *Polycera*, *Doto*, *Aplysia*, and *Actœon*. Especially in favour as an habitat for some of them is that pretty sea-weed, *Codium tomentosum*, on the leaves of which, some specimens either of *Actœon* or *Hermœa* are nearly always to be found.

The lowest animals of the molluscous class, the *Ascidians*, those curious jelly-like animals, " which live at the bottom of their own lungs," have numerous representatives in these islands, especially those social forms which live together embedded in one common mass, called *compound Ascidians*. There is scarcely one stone at St. Martin's flats, or the South-western point of Samson, which does not bear some forms of these animals. Out of thirty species recorded as British, in Professor Forbes's and Mr. Hanley's work on " British Mollusca," Dr. Carus found twenty species to be inhabitants of the Scilly Islands. He was less fortunate with regard to the simple *Ascidians*, finding only about eight species, most of them in deep water off Peninis Head, and the South coast of St. Agnes.

Marine *articulated animals*, (as Crabs and Worms), occur most generally round these islands, yet more numerous with regard to specific difference than to the frequency of specimens of a single species. A list of higher Crustacea furnished by the late Mr. Couch, will be found in the next paper ; but also some lower forms occur, though not very plentiful. Among the parasitic sucking Crustacea, (*Siphonostomata*), are some interesting species belonging to the genera *Cirolana*, *Cecrops*, *Lœmargus*, *Caligus*, &c.

And the family of sand-hoppers, water-fleas, and others,
which seem to be nothing but legs, were being forgotten,
when these lonely isles were first peopled. Only three
forms of *Cirripedia*, (Barnacles, &c.,) were noticed by
Dr. Carus, the first, a *Balanus*, which covers some of the
Western rocks entirely, and is abundant everywhere ; the
second, a pedunculated form, adhering to Corallines from
deep water ; and lastly, one out of the mouth of a sun-fish,
who had gone to sleep before it occurred to him to chew his
dessert. There were thousands of the common Barnacle
sticking to a piece of wreck at the Western coast of Annet,
but they came probably with the vessel, and do not belong
to the Fauna of this place.

The most common Worm is a species of *Nereis*, which
the fishermen use for bait, the common lugworm being
rather scarce, at least at certain times of the year. Another
species of the same genus is generally found in the roots of
laminarians, and at low-water mark, where also some of the
sedentary forms are to be found.   Dr. Carus did not find a
single specimen of the Seamouse, (*Aphrodite*), but as
representatives of the family, some species of *Polynoe*.
Some fishes furnished intestinal worms, of which *Tristoma
Molae* from the skin of the same uncouth looking Sun-fish
was the most interesting.

The next class is that of the *Echinodermata* (animals
with spinous skin.)   Among the true starfishes the
Gibbous Starlet, (*Asterina Gibbosa*), is the most common.
It is found between tide-marks everywhere. The next in
abundance is the common Cross-fish, (*Uraster Rubens*),
between tide-marks.   Rare are the spiny Cross-fish
(*Uraster Glaciallis*), the eyed *Cribella*, and the Butthorn,
(*Asterias Aurantiaca*).   The Sand and Brittle-stars are
represented by five species.   The Rosy Feather-star,
(*Comatula Rosea*), one of the finest animals which people
the sea, " whose history is a little romance," occurred only
twice in fifteen fathoms, but very frequently between tide-
marks.   There came up with the dredge one fine adult and

one young specimen of *Echinus Flemingii*, Fleming's Sea-urchin, one of the rarest British Echinoderms, from thirty-fathoms water, off Menawethan. Besides this, the Common Sea-urchin, (*E. sphæra*), and Purple Heart-urchin, (*Spatangus purpureus*), were frequently caught ; also the green Sea-urchin, (*Echinocyamus pusillus*), made its appearance frequently. The angular Sea-cucumber, (*Cucumaria pentacles*), and the Nigger or Cottonspinner (systematic name unknown,) the former more common than the latter, were found between tide-marks and in the laminarian zone. New to the British Fauna is a (*Synapte Duvernœa ?*) which was found, whilst dredging in very shallow water between St. Martins and Great Ganilly, adhering to the rope.

Medusæ seem to occur abundantly, the sea sparkling in calm nights like fluid gold.

A paper on *Zoophytes* is subjoined.

CRUSTACEA*

Many of the visitors to these islands will, no doubt, have observed, in the course of their wanderings along the sea-margin of the beaches, numerous dead crabs lying amidst the tangle of the sea-weed. These are not what they at first seem, and, in fact, are not dead crabs at all ; or not more so than the cast skin of the serpent is the serpent itself. On examination, these shells will be found to be entirely hollow, destitute of even a fragment of flesh. The eyes, the claws, the body, are the mere skins which the former owners have left to be destroyed by the winds and waves. It must be known to all, that crabs and lobsters like most other creatures, grow ; and yet, perhaps, it has rarely, if ever, occurred to the mind to enquire how that growth can be effected, seeing that the external case is so solid and unyielding. These fragments found on the shore will explain the mystery. All crabs and lobsters grow, first by casting off the hard external case, and afterwards rapidly enlarging the new one before it has become hard. In the very young, this process is effected frequently through the year ; but less so as they get older. Those of middle size do it from once to four times during the year, while in the very old it is of irregular and rare occurrence. When a crab is about to cast its shell, it becomes more

---

* This paper and the next were furnished by the late Mr. R. Q. Couch, whose premature death was lamented by all lovers of natura science.

inactive than usual ; a new skin is formed under the old
crust, and finally the old one is altogether removed from
any vital connection with the animal. During this process
the different seams become loose, and the frame fragile. In
most crabs, there is a waved seam under the front of the
back or dorsal surface, this becomes disunited and the two
edges become separated ; and this is continued quite round
to the hinder legs. This separation gradually increases,
and the animal, by imbibing sea-water, obtains a great
lever by which all the external parts become widely
separated. The animals then escape backward, leaving the
shell entire, and as the parts are elastic they then close
again, and thus it leaves the case as perfect as if the crab
still remained within. The creature, after it has escaped, is
as soft as wet parchment, and may be wrapped into any
shape. The internal parts are all present, but very indis-
tinct from this watery condition. No sooner is the animal
liberated from the old shell, than it swallows a large
quantity of fluid, and distends itself to the utmost. In
this state we have known a crab grow from one inch and a
half to two inches and one-eighth in a very few minutes.
The crabs do not remain in this soft state very long. Fresh
lime is deposited in the new skin, which in a few days
becomes as hard as that just shed. In casting the old shell,
every part of the body is renewed. The coatings of the
eye, of the stomach, blood-vessels, and the large flat
structures in the claws are left behind and reformed in the
new. If a crab has suffered an injury, or lost a claw, the
injuries are repaired, and the claws are reproduced in these
periodical renewings of youth. Notwithstanding, however,
these renovations, age will at length assert her rights, and
inflict her penalties. They lose at last their full power of
entirely shedding the shell, and hence frequently die in the
very act. This mode of growth will readily explain what
visitors will frequently find in their researches among the
rocks. In the first place, it shows why so many empty

shells are occasionally seen washed up by the tide ; in the
second, why crabs, in a soft watery state, are sometimes
found below stones, between tide-marks ; and in the last,
why the claws of crabs are so irregular in size. We could
willingly enter more particularly into interesting details on
these points, but our limits forbid.   To those who wish to
know more on the subject, we would ᐧ recommend the
Reports of the Polytechnic Society of Cornwall,* and the
History of British Crustacea, by Bell.† In these works it
will be found, that the crab, like the butterfly, undergoes a
series of metamorphoses on its passages from the egg to the
adult state. But we turn from these considerations to those
of more practical utility, especially to those who are fond of
crabs as an addition to the pleasures of the table.   ᛫

The Common, or Edible Crab, (*Cancer Pagurus*), is common from the smallest to the largest size. Those best fitted
for the table are the males, the females being rarely sought
after.   The distinction between the sexes may at once be·
ascertained, by examining the triangular flap that lies bent
on the under portion of the crab ; in the males it is
narrow, occupying the centre of the groove only, while in
the females it is widely spread even to the roots of the claws
on either side. The males only are selected for the London
market. Crabs are sometimes said to be in and out of
season, according to the solidity of the flesh ; but this can
apply only to that individual case, and not to the general
season. If the crabs and lobsters change their shells
irregularly throughout the year, there must be many both
in and out of season, during every month of the year ;
and the fluidity of the flesh depends, therefore, only on the
arrival of the period in which they may be about to cast
their shells.

Lobsters are also abundant in deep water, and are ex--
ported to the London and other markets.

* Papers by Messrs. J. and R. Q. Couch.

† Published by Van Voorst.

Prawns are to be found among the pools and between the rocks at low water, in great abundance, large quantities of which are weekly sent to the market at Penzance.

The subjoined is a list of the Crustacea discovered in the neighbourhood :—

Smaller Spider Crab...Stenorynchus longirostis, *deep water, soft ground.*

Smaller Spider Crab... Stenorynchus Phalangium, *deep water, among rocks.*

Scorpion Spider...... Inachus scorpio, *in crab pots.*

——————...... Dorynchus, *in crab pots.*

Sea Spider .... Pisa Gibsii, *crab pots.*

Corwich .... Maia squinado, *in moderately deep water.*

Furrowed Crab...... Xantho florida, *low water, under stones.*

Small Furrowed Crab ——— rivulosa, *low water, under stones.*

Crab............... Cancer Pagurus, *low water rocks.*

Furry Crab .... Pilumnus hirtellus, *under stones, low water.*

Canker .... Carcinus mœnos, *common.*

Velvet Crab........ Portunus puber, *common about tide-marks, under stones.*

Nipper Crab .... ——— corrugatus, *rare.*

Swimming Crab .... ——— depurator, *rare, taken in nets.*

Marbled Crab ...... ——— marmoreus, *deep water, nets.*

Livid Swimming Crab ——— holsatus, *fragment of shell only, at Old Grimsby.*

Swimming Nipper Crab, Polybius Henslowii, *pilchard nets, deep water.*

Angular Crab ...... Gonoplax angulata, *trawl.*

——————— ...... Planes Linnœana, *in sea-weed.*

Long Armed Crab .. Corystes Cassivelanus, *Grimsby, on the beach.*

Common Soldier.... Pagurus Bernhardus, *common*.
Hermit Crab ...... ———— Prideauxii, *old shells*.
Hermit —— ...... ———— ulidianus, *shells*.
Hermit —— ...... ———— Hyndmanni, *rare*.
Hermit —— ...... ———— lævis.
Hairy Crab........ Porcellana platycheles, *low-water, under stones.*
Hair Crab........ ——-—— longicornis, *low water.*
Plated Lobster .... Galathea squanifera, *off the shores.*
Spinous Lobster .. ——-—— strigosa.
Craw Fish........ Palinurus vulgaris, *common in deep water.*
Lobster.......... Homarus vulgarus.
Shrimp.......... Crangon vulgaris, *common.*
———— .... Hyppolyte cranchii, *crab pots, rare.*
Prawn.......... Palæmon serratus, *common.*

ZOOPHYTES.

The creatures included under the term Zoophyte are exceedingly interesting ; for though rooted and arborescent, and in many other particulars assuming the external appearance of vegetables, yet they are in reality of an animal character. It may be difficult to persuade the uninitiated of the truth of this. Fixed to their bed by roots as perfectly as any tree, with branches spreading in all directions, with buds and blossoms, and a periodic development of fruit which falls off when ripe ; with characters thus vegetable, it seems a contradiction to the evidence of our senses to suppose them to be of any other than vegetable origin. But notwithstanding all this, their animal character is undoubted. The little cups which are observed to give the zigzag appearance to the branches and stems of the horny kinds, are the habitation of the little polypes which have erected the superstructure. The polypes nestle in these cups when in a state of rest, but when taking their food, they protrude themselves from their hiding place and extend their flexible arms to catch their prey. This is no sooner done than it is conveyed to the mouth and into the stomach, where it is digested. The nourishment thus taken by each polype is conveyed to all parts of the tree by means of a central vital pulp, which connects all the polypes together. The larger cells frequently observed, are the fruit or ovarian vesicles, and

are produced in the summer and autumn, then ripen and
fall off. These cells contain small globes covered with
minute hairs, which are constantly in motion. When the
grains have escaped into the surrounding water, they whirl
themselves about, like worlds in miniature, in search of a
place on which to rest. According to the temperature is
the time thus occupied. Having settled on a fitting spot,
the hairs on the lower part become converted into roots,
and that, which was before so active and unrestrained a
creature, becomes rooted for as long a period as life shall
last. The roots below increase, and the upper parts shoot
up into the forms characteristic of each species. It would
be out of place in a work like the present to enter into the
strange eventful history of these creatures; to say how they
resist the injuries of the knife, how they can be cut up and
yet each part can become a new animal, or how they can be
turned inside out, and yet digestion will go on as well as
before; these points will be found fully described in works
dedicated to this branch of Natural History.

The species here enumerated have been taken among the
islands. In making the examination, the collector was
satisfied with a single specimen of each, and hence he did
not carefully note the frequency with which each species
occurred. There can be no doubt but that the localities in
which they may be found would have been increased, if
time had permitted a longer search, and several species will
probably be added to the list by subsequent observers. The
present enumeration, therefore, must be taken as the result
of a very limited examination, and must be considered as
only an approximation to the true number. The names
employed are chiefly those used in the third part of the
Fauna of Cornwall; and this has been done to facilitate
any reference which collectors may be desirous of making;
for in that work there is an extensive list of synonyms for
each species. Among those here enumerated is the
Gorgonia flabellum, a species found also by Dr. Borlase on
the shores of Mount's Bay. I think it must be allowed

that the specimen of Mount's Bay, and that found at Bar
Point, are foreign. Both were dead when discovered, as
well as much injured; and the great number of homeward-
bound vessels that shelter among the islands will fully
account for the occasional appearance of the species in that
locality. After extensive dredging, and examination of the
dredges of trawlers from different parts of the shores, no
living specimen has yet been discovered.

The subjoined is a list of Zoophytes found at Scilly :—

Coryne squamata, *on sea-weeds and rocks between tide-
marks. Peninnis Head, St. Mary's, St. Agnes, and
Tresco.*

Hydractinia echinata, **St. Mary's, Tresco.** *Formerly
supposed to be a variety of C. Squqmata.*

Hermia glandulosa, *on stones between tide-marks, St.
Mary's, St. Agnes.*

Tubularia ramea, *from deep water, between Samson and
Annet.*

———— indivisa, *off St. Mary's, deep water.*

Tabularia larynx, *at low water mark, on the under surface
of overhanging rocks in muddy situations, Tresco and
Samson.*

Thoa halecina, *a shell from deep water off St. Mary's.*

Sertularia polyzonias, *var. a. and b.,* with *S. Ellisii, on
shells and stones, from deep water.*

———— pumila, *between tide-marks, on fuci, St. Mary's,
Tresco. St. Agnes, and St. Martin's.*

———— tamarisca, *St. Martin's, deep water.*

———— abietina, *St. Mary's, off Old Town.*

———— filicula, *on sea-weeds, L. digitata, &c.*

———— operculata, *St. Martin's, on the stem of large
sea-weeds.*

———— argentea, *from deep water, off Kettle Point,
Tresco.*

———— cupressina, *Tresco.*

Thuiaria thuja, *fragments found on the beach at Porcressa
Bay, St. Mary's.*

Antennularia antennina. *St. Mary's.*

———·——— ramosa, *off Johnston, St. Mary's.*

Plumularia falcata, *deep water, Tresco.*

———·——— cristata, *on the stems of the larger sea-weed.*

——·——— catherina, *fragment on a shell at St. Martin's.*

———·—— frutescens, *St. Mary's.*

Laomedea dichotoma, *in pools between tide-marks.*

———·— Geniculata, *in pools.*

———·— obliqua, *a small specimen from Bryher.*

Companularia syringa, *St. Agnes.*

———·——— dumosa, *parasitical on P. falcata, Tresco.*

Gorgonia verrucosa, *from deep water.*

———·—— flabellum, *a dead specimen on the beach under Bar Point, St. Mary's.*

Alcyonium digitatum, *deep water, on shells.*

Turbinolia borealis, *on a stone from deep water; a variety, I believe, of Caryophyllia Smithii.*

———·—— Milletiana, *dredged off the coast of Scilly, by Mr. MacAndrew and Professor Forbes.*

Caryophyllia Smithii, *deep water, on stones.*

Zoagthus Couchii, *off the North of Tresco.*

Capnea sanguinea, *Tresco, deep water, on a shell.*

Corynactis viridis, *St. Mary's.*

Actinia mesembryanthemum, *pools and rocks.*

———·— margaratifera, *St. Mary's.*

———·— viduata, *Tresco, sandy places between tide-marks.*

———·— alba, *in muddy crevices.*

———·— chrysanthellum, *inlets in a sandy nook North of Tresco.*

———·— gemmacea, *var. b., Tresco.*

———·— parasitica, *deep water, on a shell.*

———·— bellis, *in pools and in crevices and muddy nooks.*

Actinia dianthus, *pools.*

Anthea cereus, *pools.*

Lucernaria auricula, *beyond low-water mark, underneath the Castle, St Mary's.*

———— fascicularis, *by Dr. Carus, at Norwithiel, on muddy stones, at low-water mark.*

Tubulipora patina, *on stones and shells from deep water, St. Martin's.*

———— hispida, *St. Martin's.*

———— penicillata, *St. Martin's.*

———— phalangea, *St. Martin's.*

———— serpens, *St. Martin's.*

———— obelia, *Tresco, from the North shore.*

———— trahens, *St. Mary's, deep water.*

Crisia eburnea, *among the roots of the larger sea-weed.*

——— cornuta, *roots of sea-weed.*

——— chelatus, *roots of sea-weed.*

Hippothoa catenularia, *on shell from deep water.*

———— cassiterides, *on a stone between the islands and Land's-end.*

Cellepora pumicosa, *on shells and stones.*

———— ramulosa, *off Annet.*

———— cervicornis, *deep water.*

Lepralia granifera, *on a stone at St. Agnes.*

———— pedilostoma, *St. Agnes, St. Mary's.*

———— reticulata, *St. Agnes.*

———— variolosa, *St. Mary's.*

———— nitida, *St. Agnes.*

———— tridentata, *St. Agnes.*

———— immersa, *St. Mary's.*

Membranipora pilosa, *var. a. and b., on sea-weed.*

———— membranacea, *on sea-weed.*

Cellularia ciliata, *on corallines and roots of sea-weed.*

———— scruposa, *among the roots of sea-weed.*

———— reptans, *among the matted roots of sea-weed.*

———— avicularia, *from deep water on the roots of sea-weed.*

Flustra foliacea, *a fragment on the Crow Bar, St. Mary's.*

———— membrancea, *on the fronds of sea-weed, as a thin gauze-like expansion.*

Eschara foliacea, *deep water.*

Retepora reticulata, *fragment on the strand at Old Town Bay.*

Salicornia farciminoides, *deep water.*

Valkeria spinosa, *on sea-weed, Tresco.*

———— cuscata, *on Sert Pumila.*

Serialaria lendigera, *on sea-weed, Tresco.*

THE GEOLOGY

OF THE

SCILLY ISLANDS.

Extracted from a Paper read before the Royal Geological

Society of Cornwall in September, 1850.

——— ———

The whole of the islands are composed of granite, and as there are no excavations worthy of the name of quarries, these remarks will apply to the granite only as it is seen on the surface.

It has been generally supposed that the granite of Scilly is a continuation of that of the Land's-end, but as in dredging between the islands and the mainland, sea-weed is often brought up attached to bits of slate or greenstone; and as the Wolf-rock, which lies not far southward of a line from the Land's-end to Scilly, is not granite, but greenstone, there is reason to believe that a tract of slate or greenstone occurs between the Land's-end and the islands, and that the granite of the latter is a separate and distinct range.

The inclination, or *strike*, of the granite of Scilly is, with few exceptions, towards the N. or N. W. This is

evident in many parts of St. Mary's, at New Grimsby in
Tresco, and particularly on the northern coast of St. Agnes
and Annet, and in most of the islands and reefs West of
St. Agnes.

In the few remarks which I can offer on this subject, I
shall refer to

I. THE JOINTED STRUCTURE OF THE GRANITE.

It is impossible to view the granite of the islands without being struck with its intersection by lines—often very
minute—in different directions : these are joints, and are
easily mistaken for cracks.   Whether they are the result
of the contraction of the granite in cooling, or owe their
existence to certain laws of crystallization, is not easy to
decide.   They are, however, more numerous at the surface
than in deeper parts, and wherever they appear, although
they may be less apparent in one part of a block than in
another, they can generally be traced throughout the
whole.

The direction of the joints appears so various and
irregular, and many of them are so crossed and curved,
that on a cursory view, it might be deemed impossible to
reduce them to any general system ; but a closer inspection
will shew that (as in most granite districts) they may be
divided into three series :— 1. Those which are horizontal, or nearly so, and parallel with what is called the *grain*
of the rock, or the direction in which it may be most
easily quarried.   In this direction the granite of the
islands is generally cloven, and the work is called " capping
and quartering. "   2.   The vertical or perpendicular joints
whose direction is generally N. and S., or perhaps N. N. W.
and S. S. E.   These, which are often inclined, may be
called the *cleavage planes*, because, in most granite districts,
the rocks are cloven in this direction, it being found in
practice the most convenient and economical. 3.   The
vertical joints having a direction varying from E. and W.
to E. N. E. and W. S. W.   These are generally inclined to

the **N.** or **N. N. W.**, parallel with the general dip, or *strike* of the granite. When the rock is thickly jointed, the inclined masses seem to repose on each other like strata of slate, as on the western side of Peninnis Head : at Water-mill Bay, the joints are so close to each other, and so highly inclined, as to give to the whole mass the appearance of stratified granite.

II. THE DISINTEGRATION AND DECOMPOSITION OF THE GRANITE.*

There is little doubt that wherever joints occur, there is the commencement of decomposition, but, according to the quality of rock, it may be rapid, or very slow: generally, by the action of the elements, the lines gradually become fissures, which, more or less rapidly, make their way into the rock, and often cause an entire separation.

1. If the vertical and horizontal joints cross each other nearly at right angles, the rocks will appear to be divided into irregular quadrangular masses (as in the western groups at Peninnis) : as decomposition proceeds, these will be gradually, and at length entirely, separated from the main body, and rounded at their edges and angles by the influence of the elements : if they are not much inclined, they may continue in their original position ; but if otherwise, they will fall from the mass, and either remain in heaps near the foot, or be rolled to a considerable distance.†
Some may continue in detached perpendicular groups, forming what are called *Tors*, (as at Carn Leh, Dick's Carn, &c.) ; and rounded insulated rocks may be so placed

---

* It is often difficult to decide whether the effects are those of decomposition or of mere disintegration. With respect to the joints, it is possible that both may be in operation, but the rounding of the sharp points of the rocks, and the formation of the rock basins, have probably been effected by disintegration.

† It is almost impossible to observe the piles of loose rocks—many of them of immense size—resting on the rocky beach between Tolmen Point and the Giant's Castle, without the conviction that they must have fallen from a higher situation.

on other rocks as to form what Dr. Borlase calls Tolmens (as the Dram rock, and a similar rock at the head of Old Town porth.) 2. When decomposition proceeds rapidly on the perpendicular joints, and has little effect on the horizontal ones, the rocks acquire a columnar form, resembling basaltic pillars, the horizontal joints answering to the joints of basalt.* 3. If the perpendicular joints are very thickly inserted in the granite, with scarcely any horizontal joints, the whole mass, as the joints yield to decomposition, appears divided into large slabs standing upright; some entirely separate, whilst others are still united at the centre : one of the best instances of this may be seen at Peninnis Head. 4. The decomposition at the horizontal joints, where there are few vertical ones, produces groups of flat tabular masses or slabs, of which the upper ones frequently protrude far beyond those on which they stand. The Pulpit rock is a fine specimen of horizontal decomposition ; others may be seen at the Blue Carn, the Clapper rocks, and in many other parts. It is possible that the Logan stones may have been formed by similar decom· position.

A more interesting effect of decomposition, or rather disintegration, appears in the Rock Basins. They are rarely seen on the rocks covered by the sea at high-water, but otherwise they are so general that the rocks, on whose surface they do not appear, form the exception. As they have been so particularly alluded to in this volume, nothing further need be said in the way of description. That they are artificial, as Dr. Borlase contends, is a doctrine now generally rejected; but a few of the facts which oppose it may be worthy of notice : some of these existed when Dr. Borlase wrote, and time has since furnished others. 1. They are deepest and most common where the rocks are most exposed to the prevailing winds and the spray of the sea. In St. Mary's, they abound on that part which

---

* This is finely exhibited in the rocks at, and south of, the Land's-end of Cornwall, especially at Tol Pedn Penwith.

extends from the S. W. to the S. E., but are few and
shallow in the other parts of the island. 2. Some of
them appear in the sides of the rocks, just as if, after they
had been formed on the top, the rocks had been over-
turned : they may be thus seen near Pitt's Parlour, at
Peninnis, and also at the Clapper rock. 3. In some cases,
when one rock is overlaid by another, basins are formed on
the lower rock : this occurs at the Clapper rock, and also
near the Sun rock, but the best instance may be seen about
a quarter of a mile north of the Sun rock, where a large
block of granite rests on another block imbedded in the
ground, the space between the two rocks being only a few
inches : on the surface of the lower rock are three regular
basins, which could not have been worked out by tools :
the top of the upper rock has also several basins. 4. The
disintegration in the basins is still proceeding : loose particles of quartz and felspar are commonly found in them,
and in several, there are openings in the sides or at the
bottom, some of which have taken place within the
recollection of persons now living. 5. On the rising
ground above Porth Loggos, there is an immense flat rock,
nearly level with the ground, said to be 173 feet long, and
138 feet wide, of which Dr. Borlase says :— " We found
the back of the rock cleaved by art (at least as it seemed
to us) of all unevenness, and making one plane of rock."
This was written about one hundred years ago : its surface
is now covered with small basins, drains, and shallow
excavations.

It is not impossible that the rock basins, as well as the
Logan stones and other natural monuments, might have
been used by the Druids for superstitious purposes, but the
facts already stated are sufficient to prove that they have
not been formed by art, but by disintegration, caused by
the alternate action of the elements on rocks peculiarly
favorable to their operation, either from a mixture of iron
or some other extraneous substance in their composition, or

from the peculiar arrangement of the crystals of the different constituent parts.

In those parts of the coast which are exposed to the prevailing winds and the lash of the waves, the rocks are weathered into the most singular and fantastic forms, as at Peninnis, and the Clapper rocks in St. Mary's, the Nag's head in St. Agnes, &c. In the latter island, some of the rocks resemble gigantic petrified mushrooms. Decomposition is also often visible on the flat surface of the rocks, as at the Lizard point in Tresco. The existence of white clay in Holy Vale moor, and in the moors between Porth Mellin and Old Town, is also an indication of it below the surface.

III. Regenerated or Secondary Granite.

There are many instances in the islands in which, at first sight, it appears doubtful whether the granite is in the process of disintegration, or whether the constituent parts which had been previously separated by disintegration, have become re-united (by what agency it is difficult to say) before they were completely decomposed. This kind may be found on Rat island, and at Piper's hole in St. Mary's ; at Piper's hole in Tresco ; and in numerous other localities. The principal reason for supposing it to be regenerated granite is that, in both the caverns alluded to, of which it forms the whole or the principal part of the roof, it contains bowlders, or rounded masses of perfect granite,—some of them pretty large : it is not easy to suppose that these could have been enclosed in original granite.

Unless these bowlders may be supposed to be the remains of ancient beaches, I have not observed on the islands any of those remains : it is not improbable, however, that they may be visible in the roofs of other caverns which I have not examined.

IV. Varieties of Granite.

The granite of Scilly is not always confined to the usual constituent parts of quartz, felspar, and mica : shorl is a very common ingredient, sometimes accompanying the mica (Lizard point, Tresco), and sometimes replacing it (Old Town porth): horneblende is a more rare one (Old Town porth), and chlorite still rarer. In some parts it is porphyritic (Watermill bay) ; but in general that term is not applicable to it : the felspar is sometimes of a deep red colour (Old Town porth,—Porth Munich,—the Cow rock.) In one locality (Lizard point, Tresco), the mica of the granite is in its primitive crystal, a sold rhomboid being formed by the accumulation of rhomboidal tables : in other parts the mica is in hexagonal tables, often forming prisms by their accumulation (Peninnis): on Taylor's island, the mica is replaced by minute prisms of tourmaline, often with a perfect termination. Binary granite, composed of only two of the usual ingredients, occurs at Porth Hellick, both as quartz and felspar, and as quartz and mica.

The granite of Scilly is, in general, of a rather course quality, and from its colour, iron appears to be frequently associated with it. No doubt there is excellent granite in several of the islands, but it is often so mixed up with what is inferior, that there is little hope of its being extensively quarried for exportation : it is possible, however, that the compact granite may run in courses or ranges through the coarser or softer kinds : this might be discovered without much difficulty by following it so far as to ascertain its direction, and examining the granite in different parts in that direction. There is very compact granite at Peninnis, but close to it there is some of a very different kind. The best, I think, may be found in some of the western islets, particularly in Rosevear, of which a specimen may be seen in the habitations of the St. Agnes lighthouse men : that of the Bishop,—the most western rock of the whole group,—is also very compact, although a little discoloured.

V. Veins in the Granite.

These are of various kinds. Sir H. De La Beche has

remarked that granite veins in the granite are not
unfrequent in St. Mary's, St. Martin's, Tresco, Brehar, and
St. Agnes: some of these, however, owe their vein-like
appearance to an accumulation of parallel joints, and the
decomposition of the granite on each side of them.   The
granite of the veins is almost always much finer than that
of the mass.   The red granite is generally found in veins
(Old Town and Brehar.)   I believe them to be all con-
temporaneous, or as nearly so as possible.

Veins of pure white quartz,—sometimes of a considerable
size,—often intersect the granite : in one of these, at Peninnis head, I found a small bunch of rose-coloured quartz :
in another vein, between St. Mary's pier and Rat island
(now covered by the new pier), chalcedony has been found.

At Watermill bay, in St. Mary's, the pebbles on the
beach indicate the contiguity of porphyry and porphyritic
granite; and on the south side of it, between the rivulet
and the curious little quay called Newquay, there is what
has been called by some an *elvan course*, and by others a
mass of decidedly stratified granite: it is of considerable
length : it rises above the granite that joins it on each side,
and seems to lie in thick strata, which are subdivided into
smaller strata, dipping at a large angle about N. N. W.:
it is decided porphyry, with small crystals of quartz and
felspar : the adjoining granite has also the same stratified
appearance.   The question is, whether the lines of division
of the apparent strata are joints, or whether the whole has
a slaty structure: the former appears to me the most
probable.   This spot must be visited at low water, or the
most interesting part will be covered by the sea.

Of metalliferous veins or lodes, there are some in three
or four of the islands, but none which any competent miner
would suppose had ever yielded any considerable quantity
of tin.   Several years ago, in digging for a foundation for
the store-keeper's house within the lines of the Garrison-
hill, a lode was discovered which produced some tin very

near the surface, but the quantity, and the lode itself, being very small, it attracted no further attention. In the small uninhabited island of Norwethel, some lodes are visible in the cliffs, and efforts have been frequently made to explore them, but unsuccessfully. In Tresco there are some lodes, on one of which, near Piper's hole, are the only remains of former works now existing in any of the islands: these, however, give no indication of extensive or important operations. Piper's hole has been called an adit for draining the mines, but it is far too irregular to admit such a supposition. Piper's hole, in St. Mary's, is more regular, and may possibly have been used for that purpose.

As so much has been already said and written on the question whether the tin of ancient times was the product of the Scilly islands, I will add only two remarks to those which I have elsewhere made on that subject. 1. Dr. Borlase supposes that a great subsidence of the land has taken place, by which almost all the marks and relics of ancient mining have been submerged; but this is not only gratuitous, but inconsistent with another conjecture of his,—that Piper's hole, in Tresco, was the adit of the ancient tin work there: if it were so, it is evident that no subsidence of the land can have taken place since. 2. There are two tracts of low land in St. Mary's: one, extending from Porth Mellin to Old Town; the other, from Holy Vale to Porth Hellick. In Tresco also there is a low tract from New Grimsby, by the Abbey ponds, to the south-east side of the island. Now, if any mines here had ever been productive of tin, some traces of diluvial tin would, even in modern days, be found in these low grounds; but in neither of them has any tin-ore ever been discovered, as far as can be known from the testimony of the living, or the records of the past; neither has any tin-ore ever been found pulverized amongst the sands of the sea shore, as it frequently is in the mining parts of Cornwall which border on the sea; I see no reason, therefore, to alter the opinion expressed elsewhere,* that the tin of the Cassiterides could not have been the product of the Scilly islands, but was probably that of the nearest land—St. Just, which, being visible from Scilly, might easily have been taken for a large island, and included in the group to which was given the name of the Cassiterides.

VI. THE SANDS OF THE ISLANDS.

These are more diversified than might be expected in such a small tract. Those which are found on the southern coasts are generally coarse and gravelly, as at Porth Hellick, Old Town porth, and Porth Cressa, whilst those on the northern shores are usually very fine, as at Porth Mellin and the Pool. The sand of Porth Mellin is the most interesting of the whole : here, at low water, on the surface of the beach, which is composed of almost impalpable particles of quartz,—so fine as to be generally used for scouring household utensils,—may be seen ridges of black mica : they are not always in the same situation, but are moved about by the tide : there is very little mica, and that in the minutest particles, below the surface of the sand. The granite of Carn Thomas, which adjoins this porth on the west, contains black mica, and at the foot of the carn the granite appears to be decomposing : this, however, will not account for so much being found on the beach at Porth Mellin, while in many other coves, where the granite around them is similarly composed, scarcely any mica can be seen on the sands : it is difficult to conjecture how, after the dissolution of the felspar and the minute reduction of the quartz, the mica should have remained, in larger particles, on the surface : is it possible that a gentle current may convey it there from some other part ? Eastward, the sand of the Bar is quartzose, but less fine, with a very small admixture of shell : in the sand of Pellestry bay alone is there a mixture of comminuted shells sufficient to make it very useful for manure : other sands are

* Cornwall Geol. Trans., Vol. 2, page 357.

frequently used for that purpose, but their principal virtue is probably that of loosening close or clayey soils.

On the southern side of Tresco, the sand consists almost entirely of large particles of pure white quartz, which might probably be used in the manufacture of porcelain, instead of pounded flint; but I am not aware that it has been tried.

It will be observed that in this communication I have said nothing of St. Martin's island, or of the eastern islands, and little of Brehar, or Samson. In truth, I had not sufficient time to examine them: they must be left for another " week's visit to the islands."

ROWE, PRINTER, BOOKSELLER, &c., PENZANCE.